THE SECRET OF THE EMPIRE

Studies in Austrian Literature, Culture, and Thought

Translation Series

Heimito von Doderer

The Secret of the Empire

A Novel of the Russian Civil War

Translated and with a Foreword
and an Afterword
by
John S. Barrett

ARIADNE PRESS
Riverside, California

Ariadne Press would like to express its appreciation to the Austrian Cultural Institute, New York and the Bundeskanzleramt – Sektion Kunst, Vienna for their assistance in publishing this book.

Translated from the German *Das Geheimnis des Reichs*
Excerpted from *Frühe Prosa*

Library of Congress Cataloging-in-Publication Data

Doderer, Heimito von, 1896-1966.
[Geheimnis des Reichs, English]
The secret of the empire : a novel of the Russian Civil War / Heimito von Doderer ; translated and with a foreword and an afterword by John S. Barrett.
p. cm. -- (Studies in Austrian literature, culture, and thought. Translation series)
ISBN 1-57241-061-2 (pbk.)
1. Soviet Union--History--Revolution, 1917-1921--Fiction.
2. World War, 1914-1918--Prisoners and prisons, Austrian--Fiction.
3. Austrians--Soviet Union--History--20th century--Fiction.
4. Prisoners of war--Soviet Union--Fiction. I. Barrett. John S. (John Smith), 1935- . II. Title. III. Series.
PT2607.03G4413 1998
833'.912--dc21

98-14097
CIP

Cover Design:
Art Director, Designer: George McGinnis

270 Goins Court
Riverside, CA 92507

Printed in the United States of America.
ISBN 1-57241-061-2 (paperback original)

This translation is in honor of

Dr. Engelbert Pfeiffer

Curator of the Doderer Memorial Rooms
Bezirksmuseum Alsergrund, Vienna

Foreword

The impressions of modern Russia gained from day to day reading and television reports are much like those experienced on a ride through the house of horrors in an amusement park: illuminated tableaus, some terrifying, some merely bizarre, suddenly leap out, then are swallowed up again by the darkness which holds sway until another set of images flashes out to demand one's total attention, blotting out memories of what went before and making it difficult to think about what might lie ahead. The display of Russia before us just now is dominated by the huge figures of Yeltsin, the Mafiosi, and the crass new rich, displayed against a backdrop of economic chaos, poverty, despondency, and anger. The man with the birthmark on his forehead who changed the world has been engulfed by darkness. Somewhere back there, behind the fur-hatted, old men waving mechanically from the Kremlin walls, behind blinking sputnik, before the man with the mustache and all those dead bodies, was a revolution and, as Doderer's subtitle reminds us, a civil war.

While the several excellent histories now available bathe that earlier era in uniform and revealing light, the writers and playwrights of those times – though admittedly more random and subjective in their approach – provide a view of Russia that may inform us differently and perhaps affect us more strongly than formal histories, much like the narrow beam of a flashlight probing through the darkened house of horrors, momentarily revealing the cracked papier maché face of what was thought to be a terrifying monster, or cobwebs, paper cups, and dead mice at the feet of some beneficent-appearing giant. Isaak Babel's diaries and fiction capture the awfulness of the early cavalry battles in a particular and insidious way; Mikhail Bulgakov's *The Master and Margarita* makes the reader a fellow sufferer in the paranoid – and sometimes hilarious – lunacy of Stalin's Moscow. In like fashion, Doderer's *Secret of the Empire* illuminates the fate – sometimes terrible, sometimes less bad, often astonishing – of some of the many thousands of Austrian soldiers captured by the Russians in World War I and shipped off to prison camps in Siberia. It is another odyssey after another war, played out not on the wine dark sea, but along the Trans-Siberian Railroad.

The booming voice of Doderer's offstage narrator and the actions of his characters revive and relive what we once knew vaguely about the First World War in the east and the Russian Revolution that followed, but also bring to our attention what we may not have known: that disease killed perhaps half of the several hundred thousand captured Austro-Hungarians, yet the prison camps had walls that were not totally confining and that theaters, coffee houses, libraries, as well as cottage industries and fraudulent capitalistic endeavors, all flourished; that enlisted men might be worked to exhaustion and death by their captors, but officers still might draw pay or find work outside the prison camp; and that the Russians could be thought of sympathetically, kindly, even fondly, by enlisted men and officers alike.

But destiny has suspended the prisoners between two

opposing forces that threaten their destruction: from one side, the Russian Civil War – once a distant event hardly even noticed by the local peasants and the Austrians – advances inexorably from European Russia toward Siberia, like a gloomy red glow on the horizon; and on the other side are the seventy thousand and more Czech prisoners, now armed and ready to be returned to battle against their former Austro-Hungarian and German masters as the "Czech Legion." However, when Trotsky, then Minister of Defense of the soviet state, decrees that the Czechs must surrender their arms as a condition for transport out of Russia, or be shot, they – rather understandably – refuse, rebel, and in the act of attempting to force their way out of Russia via Vladivostok, ally their often vicious fighting skills with those of the various White Russian armies. The Austrians, soon the targets of revenge on the part of the Czechs as well as the objects of the suspicion of their Russian captors that they might side with the advancing Communists, are transported even further east into Siberia at the moment when they are to be sent home following the conclusion of the peace treaty between Russian and the Central Powers.

But all of that, including the author's rather striking insights into the real nature of the Russian Revolution and his early use of the term "iron curtain," is history. To help understand how he put that history to use in the service of literature, however, it may useful to jump ahead, for the moment, some two decades to 1951, when Doderer put his novelistic cards on the table, so to speak, with the publication of *The Illuminated Windows, or, the Humanization of the Bureaucrat Julius Zihal.* Here, the civil servant Zihal carries into his retirement the aura of his workaday world of rules, regulations, codes and laws, all numbered and categorized – part of that whole incarcerating traditional, social, and ideological carapace of civilization that Doderer had begun to call the "second reality" – and applies it to his leisure time activity of voyeurism. Zihal's new telescope serves the second reality, rather than life, as he carefully notes down which building he's spying on, the floor and window, the time of night, the angle of inclination of the telescope, rather than really enjoying the female delights he's staring at. Until, that is, one of the women he's been observing – the opulent Rosa Oplatek – hears that he has fallen ill and comes to his aid. Amor vincit omnia: humanized, he abandons his sterile pastime and the two live happily ever after.

The Secret of the Empire, published in 1930, also examines the theme of humanization, but from a different angle: against the huge, ominous backdrop of the Russian Civil War, in the stage setting of a prisoner of war camp with its own social microcosm, the Austrian soldiers are doing battle with a different sort of "second reality," one at the opposite end of the spectrum from Zihal's. This second reality is not the prison of sterile ideologies, laws, and paragraphs, but the equally confining act of bobbling along through life like a cork, heedless of the fact that this, too, lacks full humanity. Some of the prisoners never attempt to rise above their confinement, their work, their eating, sleeping, smoking, singing, and, when possible, womanizing; some, like the author's alter ego René Stangeler, seem at first to withdraw into the role of onlooker, storing experiences for further use in their personal odysseys on the way from soldier to writer.

It is the character Jan Alwersik who exemplifies the problem most fully. Resourceful and adaptable, he is still essentially just floating down the stream of life – actually, it was a ride down the river in a kayak that made him decide to abandon his study plans and go into the army. He stands out as a seemingly strong figure among his fellow prisoners, partially because of his ability to go with the current and make the most use of whatever turns up, a situation or a human being. In an unthinking, instinctive way he becomes the lover of the wife of a Polish officer, but then uses her to cloak his activities as a Red Army scout and thus contributes unintentionally to her horrible death at the hands of a Red inquisitor. Finally realizing his iniquity, he attempts suicide, but is foiled by Stangeler, with whom he eventually escapes from Russia on foot.

Those who are unable to drift off confidently with the current of events for better or, like the character Hugo Blau, for worse, occupy themselves with a somewhat pathetic rationalization in order to subdue the horror of their imprisonment and possible eventual death far from their homeland – the drawing of comparisons between aspects of their current lives and those "back there." Things are not really so different, they try to tell themselves, the earth is the same, the snow is the same, the rivers run into the distance, in fact around the world and eventually back to their own country. Even their activities here are quite similar to the way they did things back there, in Vienna. Until, that is, typhus brings them back to grim reality as it begins to kill some of them again. In a later book Doderer would look back and say of René that he was "trying to bring dissimilar circumstances, appearances, and events under the all-confining power of comparability, which is the only thing that can bring order to all those threads of memory that are otherwise being constantly torn apart." Then, as if to cast a wistful, fatherly smile at such psychological defense mechanisms summoned up to maintain at least the semblance of humanity in the face of adversity: "Memory was important to René, recollections – that's how young he was!"

At the end of this book, the young survivors are left with inchoate personalities, but there is hope that they will develop a fuller humanity despite the heavy hand of fate and despite a set of Jungian, ingrained deterministic images within each of them. By no means inchoate, but already fully developed as presented in this early work, however, are Doderer's descriptive powers, used to document the vastness and beauty of the landscape of Russia, which constantly astonished him and his fellow prisoners, as well as his almost religious and perhaps somewhat romanticized feeling for the Russian peasants as the embodiment of the true soul of Russia. The language may at times seem effusive by our standards. But although the Vienna from which Doderer came and to which he returned after his imprisonment was, and to a certain extent still is, a place of flourishes and occasional bombast, both literary and social, it was Russia – as he later recounted – that had put him into a state of euphoria. And its cold, its clarity, and its memories held him in thrall to the end of his life.

John S. Barrett

One

Out there: sun, and houses tossed out like dice which, mixed with the countless noises of human activities, hurry off toward the horizon without rhyme or reason. But here, in this direction, starting somewhere, it is I, myself, with the solitude and the purple of my inner life.

You look – what does that all mean? I have been physically alive for thirty two years. Everything within me is a single torment and was never anything else. They live. He looks. You are tired. Contemplated calmly it is – nothing.

You walk and we meet each other. Your face inclines toward me, a year, a day. Every day disintegrates into the parts which it encompasses. The wind rises; one does not see it, but now it strikes my cheek, which feels it, or a bush, which rustles.

Sometimes in this situation, sometimes in that – and each one is stronger than the synthesis of both – sweetly, in the gray of the waning evening, from the farthest corner of the landscape where lights are twinkling, dreams draw near to the sound of pipes.

There the grass of the steppe begins, runs off toward its distant border with dark strips of forest; thrown together over there, the village with its herds. The brown earth parched, the hilltops sharp and foreign.

Wooded mountains rise up. The sky is blue. Horses are being hitched to the wagons – the tribe is about to migrate again with all its herds. The language with the dry, chattering sounds of the distant, stretched-out east. The stringy manes of the small, tough horses are tossed by the wind that comes from the opposite horizon, where the steppe with its brown hills begins to wander, far and deep into itself, to a place where one can no longer even see the mountains and their forests; only there does this people really feel at home.

The wooden plow in the hands of eastern peoples – smiled at indulgently but disparagingly by some German farmer cast up in a foreign land – and the miseries of school days, to which later life is so similar. The former were confined to one or two rooms but later, life revolves around rooms, streets, groups of people. Close by is a park; close by, my jacket is hanging over the back of a chair. The young man starts to tremble because his lover has already entered the innermost ring of proximity, so that she – gigantic in his eyes – covers the horizon even through really just a tiny object, in the same fashion as anger or fear – or something trifling – or the coal bill – just trifles. There on the sideboard in the dining room stood a genuine antique Russian tea service, vivid crimson, with a sugar bowl in a wild, barbarian shape with a brick-red zigzag pattern – "like an exotic, gruesome house somewhere in the east, a house or temple where people are killed, sacrificed, oh, something gloomy, foreign, hard, in a gigantic, sandy country where all the faces look the same . . ." That was what the little girl often thought. And then we really do get to see the temples in the east or the farms of northern Germany, have them right in front of our eyes, and we place that temple servant in the east and the proud homebody of a farmer in the north indescribably far away from the deep and serious pain of the boy over a broken little whip. All that is within us is like a remnant, like the undigested balls of fur that birds of prey regurgitate. In those balls are to be found the eastern and the northern plowmen, rooms, streets, and circles of friends . . .

Here Dorian had – in that bright upstairs room whose windows looked far out across the Danube canal and allowed one to see much that was so very distant, so tiny – here he almost always had the same taste in his mouth that he had every summer on arrival at his parents' country house: you've walked into the bright room, from all sides distance and light are pouring in through the windows, the air tastes fresh, your suitcase is standing in the corner. But then things separate: here, there was no suitcase in the corner; it lay within your own breast, an awkward thing which, slavishly dependent on the light footsteps going back and forth in the next room, was pushed back and forth depending on whether those steps approached the door. Often his heart did a needless flip-flop and she didn't come into the room. Didn't she know he was there, waiting for her brother – for whom, fortunately, one always had to wait half an hour, who, fortunately, was almost never to be found at home? But, of course, she really had to know, he came to see him almost every other day – they always did their homework together.

The transfer of Medical Corpsman Alois Dvorak from Bruck on the Leitha to Decin was effected with distinction, contrary to every expectation. The fact was that one night shortly before, Dvorak, despite being on guard duty, had left the camp and had gone into town. As the devil would have it, however, the captain who was responsible for making the rounds of the camp just had to stick his nose into the very barracks where Dvorak was to have given him the nightly report – which, of course, didn't happen, since the latter was occupied elsewhere and doubtless in a completely different fashion as well. The captain went into a rage. A quarter of an hour later, as Dvorak was about to sneak back into the barracks again as inconspicuously and soundlessly as an owl, the waves stirred up by the event were still running high; the officer had just left the scene. Dvorak's comrades were outdoing themselves in their descriptions of the disciplinary action that the corpsman would certainly face on the following day.

Dvorak walked up to the front of barracks, stood there in the dark. Here he thought things over long and carefully. And the guardian angel of common soldiers did not desert him, but actually descended upon him and provided him with an inspiration that was precisely suited to the brains of his superiors.

He walked the considerable distance over to the wall enclosing the military base, near which, alone and off to the side, stood the isolation pavilion for infectious diseases. That pavilion, though empty, had just recently been completely readied for patients and equipped with bedding and all the other necessities. Dvorak took off a boot, pushed in a window pane with it, walked back, and went to bed.

On the following day, he was chewed out during roll call. When he was finally ordered to speak up and give his side of the story, he reported in a plain, firm, and trustworthy tone that it had been unavoidably necessary to leave the barracks and carefully investigate the area around the newly equipped isolation pavilion. Suspicious noises had alerted him; and, in fact, as he approached, two men climbed over the wall and ran away – he, Dvorak, after them, though to no avail because of the darkness and their considerable head start.

Three officers took themselves off to the isolation pavilion. There the smashed-in pane was found as testimony to the truth of the corpsman's statement. Dvorak was commended for his vigilance while on guard duty.

Herr von Stefani put his razor down, but a sudden fit of distraction caused him to remain frozen in position in front of the mirror by the window, his hand raised. The sounds of automobile horns drifted up from Kärntnerstrasse as well as the lively clip-clop of hoofs, since back then horse-drawn carriages still drove through the streets of Vienna. Across the street was the opera house. The sun was on the decline, the spring day blazed up one last time, the higher window panes took on a glow; off to the right was a sharply slanting, reddish band of light. Distraction was an unusual condition for Stefani despite his youth. When he spoke, he had a squeaky voice. The fact that later in his life he would wear a red goatee – which actually turned out to be the case – was still far removed from his present smooth-shaven state. The feeling of distraction lasted a long time. Spring can have strange effects in Vienna. He asked himself what was going on, or what might still be facing him today. So far, nothing had happened. After closing time, when he'd left the ministry, he'd simply gone for a stroll, had wandered around, spending the afternoon completely differently and in completely different places than was his custom. The sudden, episodic heat of the spring – the bright green leaping up like flames here and there, from gardens, from courtyards, and long corridors of alleyways – all that had made him uneasy and had driven him onward through the streets. Stefani had come loose a bit from his usual attachments. The afternoon seemed as if it had been torn loose and was standing there all by itself. And now, that evening, he was going to go to the opera – Rigoletto.

At the opera, where Stefani was by then dressed in his tuxedo and sitting in the parquet as befit his status, there was an incident shortly before the close of the performance – a popping noise in a loge. Not really all that loud, but still clearly recognizable as a gunshot. The house became just a little restive, only to the extent of row upon row of turned heads. In the corridors afterward, it was said that someone had shot himself. A fourteen-year-old student from the Gymnasium. Stefani was actually relieved. He had indeed known that something or other was going to happen. Thank God the blow had not landed on him, but, so to speak, far away. On the following day it was all there in the newspaper. The student's name was Camillo Stökl.

13

The image that the boy René Stangeler has of the spaces around him is blurred and indistinct because of the still childishly exaggerated closeness of his immediate environment. He does not properly assign the structures of the city to the spaces in which they belong. As yet the features of alleys, the length of the streets, the size of the city's squares, and the streetcar lines and those of the subways and buses and their combinations have not been roughed out and rolled smooth within him, have not yet become habitual pathways and automatisms, certainly far from the habitual gesture that shows the ticket and the practiced boarding from the right platform; and it would have been completely impossible for him – something mutely and half-consciously familiar to us adults – to experience that already developed annoyance at all those habitual things, that hatred so ready to react against all those things – even if that hatred within us is never carried to its endpoint, flooded over as it is by the current of the day, the obligations of the day, in fact by the very handshake that engenders yet another handshake . . .

He, the boy, however, can only imagine the neighborhoods he does not know; they always have to be on the opposite side of the city, exactly opposite that district in which the overly near, overly large house of his parents stands. It has to be bright over there, totally bright, related to the vivid green of spring and related to him, himself, and his hazy, boy's life, but only as the nearest horizon, the edge of his field of vision, which could sometime be walked up to – glowing with newness. Even though scarcely understood, even though beyond the edge of vision, yet as near as anything else in the world. . .

There's the downhill slope of the park I've walked through, whose perfect, robust-soft carpet of lawn still reaches into my imagination from back then, still floods into the back of my brain, or ebbs away and flows backward, as if I were dragging a long cloak behind me. There the park falls away, down the slope of the hill, becomes tiny there below, directly in front of me, runs together into a rond-point. Standing there are little trees with crooked branches, forming corridors; indeed, wandering in those corridors, life seems really different from elsewhere, and again different in each individual leafy corridor; one can only see out through the larger or narrower spaces between branches to the place over there where everything runs together – strength, mass, and weight . . .

Because over there the eye plunges into a veritable war: the foreground of one's field of vision is crisscrossed by the bold, thick, diagonal bands of the viaducts of the elevated railway, with the winter fog suspended among them already. Beneath and through them howl the trolleys. There, standing like some gloomy lord, the giant cylinder of the gasometer, crossed in front, close up, by two tiny tree branches. Farther on, however, things become wild, the rooftops high, fire walls tossed together; below, one very low roof. Beyond – and now no longer to be restrained – things break loose: a rush of houses, a tumult of houses, a mass of houses, already blurred, a sea of houses in the fog, rolling, hurrying away. Over there to the left, gray distance and boats riding calmly at anchor; and as if that were not enough, the railroad bridge with its four arches goes caterpillaring across the stretched out ribbon of the river.

15

In the summer, after passing his final exams, Jan Alwersik was invited to his sister's place in a Galician garrison town on the San. The river attracted him all the more since there was a kayak, a tiny, light boat in which one lay rather than sat, with a paddle. The speed he could reach traveling downstream was more beautiful than any dream. At that point, a nearly insurmountable wall insinuated itself between him and his plan to attend the Foreign Trade Academy in Vienna that fall. Out on the river one time, that became palpably clear to him as he went gliding close to the shore beneath the massive canopy of trees, through the shade of their leaves and the dancing beams of sunlight. A peasant girl was bathing there; she fled up the embankment, Jan turned onto the shore, ran after her - soon they were both laughing. The bushes were as thick as a wall. As he walked out afterward, he saw the low and undulating land moving off in a thousand-mile leap under its burden of sun, and then he was violently moved as he stood there thinking to himself that it really almost ran around the earth, always the same, yet unspeakably far away! His jaw muscles tensed a little. The girl had run away, ashamed; he was scarcely thinking about her any longer and jumped into the kayak. Yes, just go on row-row-rowing your boat! He felt so relaxed recently, so to speak, just standing in his shoes, relaxed walking, relaxed here in the boat, relaxed in the girl's arms, as if he could simply step out of all that, stand beside his shoes, let the girl go her way and not touch her with a single thought, get out of the kayak there and let the thing glide off by itself, faster and faster downstream, from the San into the Vistula, and then into Russia and back out again to Germany. The land was the same everywhere, flowing away uninterruptedly.

Not long afterward, Jan kissed the business career goodbye and became an officer.

Then there was a rather remarkable time – several weeks – when Dorian suddenly met her frequently. It often turned out that they ended up together two or three days in a row. Had they really not arranged it that way? This entire rather remarkable time had perhaps not lasted several weeks, but, altogether, just a few days. In any event, the high point was when they even went on an outing together – he shivered and trembled for a long time at the thought that on this particular morning, just to meet him, she'd gone to a certain streetcar stop at a certain hour, where she could really only meet him, since no one else ever waited there. She had actually come to him! Her dress was pink. The picket fence out in the country, however, in front of which he could still see her standing later, was freshly painted white, with bright, sparkling palings. Certainly that had been the high point, just the way she'd stood in front of the white picket fence, and not things much more tangible, like when they'd lain on top of the hill at the edge of the woods, when the evening had shrunk down to a narrow, deep red glow at the edge of the sky. He'd kissed her hand, even her arm, but she'd suddenly pulled away because of a cracking noise in the underbrush, and right afterward a man came out of the woods and walked by them and down past the meadow with a relaxed, indolent stride – a stranger with a heavy, dark outline in the late dusk . . . It was a most remarkable time, full of pain as well, it was unendingly sad for the most part and he worshiped its sadness. But something was missing there: Dorian was sent to another Gymnasium in one of the provinces, because he kept failing in school; he heard nothing from her, but wanted to hear – at any rate, early on. He wrote, page after page, imploringly. Then a letter finally came from her – but here, too, something was missing. Is it possible that the letter made no impression on him by that time? By then something must have changed, because he didn't answer the letter, put off answering, and finally gave up and heard nothing further – her letter had been foreign and somehow even too "ladylike" and much too adult . . . "probably a lot will change in my life now . . ." And by then there were new friends, especially one to whom he'd felt attracted, often with a certain fine torment, which, for every pain, for every offense given, opened wide portals – indeed for almost nothing else; and after each hidden impulse, in confessions which might sweeten the burden – yet, in the end, as it all ebbed away, there was already the soft but firm voice of mistrust! This pain was probably similar to the one experienced once long ago, because of a broken little whip; nevertheless, he kept both widely separated from each other. At times things just hung within him like a mixture of leftovers that congealed and then got baked without ever having been mixed together properly. All sorts of junk could be found there: rooms, streets, circles of friends, that massive white picket fence, and that bright, upstairs room, and even quite everyday things, like his attempt, standing at the sink, to knead several scraps of toilet soap together into a nice, round ball so they could be reused . . .

The booming of high explosive shells that had lasted fourteen hours suddenly abated and was immediately replaced by the violent crackle of the shrapnel that was now bursting just above the completely destroyed trenches. Among the dead, those who were still alive struggled to their feet, reached for their rifles, threw themselves against the front of the trenches and, with their shoulders hunched together, began to fire, because now the charge was starting. At first caps, shoulders, the points of bayonets – many fell, but new ones kept coming – and then, out there in the wheat field in front of the barbed wire entanglement, the gray-green mass became denser and then very dense, trampled the wire, cut, and jumped. Hand grenades went flying out in high arcs. But the defenders, after the martyrdom of a fourteen-hour bombardment to which they had been exposed in shallow, freshly-dug trenches, soon lost their heads. Incited and misled by several young officers, they suddenly sprang out of their trenches here and there, roaring like animals, and ran forward into the enemy with their bayonets lowered. And as a result, the front – despite momentary success – tore apart and afterward three Austrian battalions were cut to pieces and the small groups surrounded by the Russians and taken prisoner . . . Every man became aware of the completely different smell of the enemy soldiers during hand-to-hand combat. Each one saw the battle raging through the hilly expanse of the landscape now, exactly as in old battle scenes – with men charging back and forth in the foreground and columns of smoke and fire in the distance and with thousands, many thousands, of individual details.

Out of the deep gloom of a winter night scarcely accessible to the imagination, with storms and thirty degrees below zero, a warm, bright cell sends forth its glow, faintly at first, then more distinctly, hovering closer and closer – there is even a samovar steaming away here. Of necessity and as a matter of course, they have turned entirely away from the landscape and into this bright, warm interior; there's not the least need to go out at all, to worry about going out, to even think about the outdoors – everything is brought in. Obviously there have to be people who bring everything out from the town, who take care of those things, but that's the Russians' business, you didn't drag yourself all the way out there to a Siberian prison camp – so let them provide what they're obliged to for officers who've been taken prisoner. You know, of course – or could know – that out there in the watch towers around the camp the guards are standing in the cold; but you don't give that the slightest thought . . . once the seasons change and warm weather comes and then the hot summer, the endless countryside, the blue mountains off in the distance and bathing – under guard – in the gigantic river that seems like a flowing ocean – then you've got it even better. Meanwhile, it's just like being pulled back into reserve positions, but without the duties and all the other things that go with that. Several have managed eventually to make some connections, have found jobs, have gotten themselves transferred out of the camp, thanks to their Russian sponsors. But there was absolutely none of that at first – officers were kept in strict confinement – and even later, it was still considered by certain people to be suspect, to be an unworthy attempt at assimilation. Those whose sure instinct told them that another opportunity would soon present itself, studied Russian in the meantime. Others stubbornly refused . . .

And so one soon turns away from the frozen windowpanes and the landscape that lies beyond them, foreign and huge and cold and inaccessible because of the snowdrifts – and thus is not really present, merely an assumption. From there one turns toward the accessible and lighted interior space and simply settles in. It suits some just perfectly that they do not have to live through this time; they discover the treasure for itself and begin carefully to unpack the gift within the time that is a gift, and they become so absorbed by this joy that the cord that leads from them to the outside withers, dries up, and falls apart like a burned fuse. Warm it is, around hearth and samovar, the evening conversations stimulating and exciting – existence worthy of a human being, without doubt; and at the same time, one is bathed by the suffused light of martyrdom and knows that one, as a poor prisoner, is held in serious respect by the whole world. With such a lack of burdens, one can happily help the flowers of intellect to blossom freely and rule the world like some minor king, against whom one cannot raise a finger; and that sort of delight in things is to be found mostly among the younger men . . . Others simply feel – and are – stopped in their tracks, set outside time and action; they can't make a thing out of this entire situation – can't make anything out of their environment, can't work enchantment on those rooms and bunks and silent evening candles and those comrades and that entire situation – on the contrary, all of that seems to set itself against them in a completely puzzling and totally annoying way. They are simply waiting. They may well go along a little with that "intellectual life" that is developing in the camp, but they don't try to use it to their advantage or have a bit of harmless fun with it, and they don't have the slightest intention of conquering the world from there, as it were, since that would appear ridiculous to them a priori; while those others, especially the young ones, think they're at a decisive point right now.

In the gigantic camps, on the other hand, where the captured enlisted men live stacked on top of one another in bunks without bedding or covers, the road is a good deal bumpier, because the Russian state is squeezing every bit of work out of those men that can possibly be squeezed out. The rapidly expanding camp cemetery receives the worn-out material. Since it has to be used till it's worn out, it's impossible to just get rid of it right off and so, here and there, someone makes it out of the gray, stinking mass of humanity somehow, finds an opportunity, a smoother road, and his own individual life again – and behold: for many, things soon begin to go splendidly. In the enlisted men's camps, everyone – unless an absolute idiot – speaks Russian.

"Those who have perished: in the military district of Olonieck, 10,000 out of 40,000 prisoners, mainly of scurvy. The rest will be lifelong cripples. In Tockoe, near Samara, more than 9,000 out of 17,000 died of typhus. In the military district of Tobolsk 2,000 prisoners were accommodated in earthen barracks; all died of typhus. In the earthen barracks at Orenburg where prisoners were housed, an American physician – who was able to make his way there only with considerable difficulty – established that 50 per cent were tubercular, 40 per cent blind. In Skobelev more that 3,000 men died in the course of two months. In Samarkand and Turkestan more than 5,000 prisoners perished of malaria . . . In Siberia, in Novo-Nikolaevsk[1] to be exact, of the 15,000 prisoners who had been in the camp for three months, 8,000 succumbed to a typhus epidemic, as well as several physicians and 27 medical students. In Krasnoyarsk, 5,000 out of 12,000 died of typhus as well. According to the statistics kept by Dr. Bauer in the camp at Verkhne-Udinsk, there were 4,000 fatalities among 30,000 prisoners over the course of a year, even without an epidemic.

They were located here and there in that gigantic country, those camps, erected mostly by boarding off a part of the "Voyenny-Gorodok," the "little war town," in other words, the barracks district. Almost every larger city along the Trans-Siberian Railroad had such an appendage – especially since the Russo-Japanese War – because at that time housing for the troops, supply depots, and armories had to be built all along the railroad line, or the already existing ones enlarged. Some of those red brick structures now stood there surrounded by plank fences. For the citizens of the city, that district was merely an

[1] Now called Novosibirsk

inclusion – through the cracks one could see foreigners in foreign uniforms and even hear them chattering away in their foreign language, if one happened by chance to walk by. For those closed in there, however, it was a structured world.

For those closed in, man for man, soul for soul, it was the time of their lives, and yet many of them at first considered this time merely a pause, a pause after having had their breath knocked out by a detonation that hurled them out of their lives – whose spaciousness not everyone had comprehended – and into a new, unheard-of situation. Many indeed believed that at first. Nevertheless, they soon got their breath back and realized, in part brazenly, in part deeply astonished, that they were swimming along in the same river as before. Many took a long time to come to this "realization" (to wit, that the landscape of their homeland in the west really did run right on to where they were now, without interruption or bottomless space in between, so that, really, despite all those events and having had their breath being knocked out, they should have done better at recognizing the earth, the snow, and the water again!) and only with this "realization" did they again become capable of the basic little tricks, in other words, went off on a detour, to a certain extent, that others were not about to travel. There were also emphatic Europeans, who in their exile surrounded themselves rather demonstratively with unfulfilled demands, for instance Herr Fleischhanger and Herr Hampe – one was a high school principal, the other a magistrate. Those two wished it to be known that they were dilettantes when it came to poverty.

A house like that in an abundance of sun, a sky that arches over to the forested hills, the coming warmth, the hot summer, the endless country, the dry woodiness of the planks, and the blueness above the distant prospect – a life like that, whether active or lost in thought, along the edges yet constantly close to some inner danger or other . . . the blue glycinias in the arbors along the playing fields add their deep color to the distance and quiet of the sunny afternoon as well . . . six small rooms on the ground floor enter onto a long and broad glass addition in front. This wing of the building is called "the veranda."

In the midst of this stillness, Ensign Stangeler is sitting on his bunk. A small wooden table is standing in front of him; on it are lying some of his daily attempts at writing. That occupation seems to be a strain for him, because he closes his eyes again and again. After two hours he has a happy expression on his face, pulls on his soccer shoes, and runs out. In the evening coolness they play a match and afterward, as Stangeler is leaving the field along with others, someone who'd just spoken with the Russians comes along and says that the camp is going to be broken up; at least some of the inmates will be transferred elsewhere (there are often such rumors, called "latrines" since they are spread, for the most part, in the expanded, multiseated outhouses during a leisurely evacuation). General cursing, shouting: "These damn latrines!" "You never get a chance to rest, I'm in the twelfth camp already!" "We're going to lose everything again!" – the man means the tables, chairs, and the like, scrounged up or improvised at the cost of considerable exertion. Then there is a discussion of the war which Kerensky is continuing to carry on; they talk guardedly and seriously, believing that almost anything could still happen, in this Russia – things that they hadn't even let themselves think about – but at any rate it was going to be a long time before they could just sit in peace and quiet, here in the camp . . .

Stangeler is walking; his heartfelt wish is to sit in peace and quiet, and not just because of the tables and chairs. The veranda is empty, his room as well – his two comrades have gone off to one of the larger halls where the newspapers that have been translated into German are read aloud each evening. Darkness is coming on; he lights a candle – there stands the table, the little manuscript is lying on it. The rumor is bothering him. At the same time, his body is intrusively animated from being on the playing field, his blood fresh and coarse. What was that he heard again? What was going on again? In Russia? Constant unrest, constant confusion! No, he'd never been to one of those newspaper readings. A bit of luck that he'd been given quarters in one of the smaller rooms by Albert Lehnder – the inhabitants of the larger halls had to put up with that disturbance each and every evening . . . Albert Lehnder was still living with Stangeler at that time; Johann von Valoisky was the third one in their chamber.

Lehnder was the camp librarian. The books had been stored in the "veranda," thus providing Albert with a good reason for approaching the commander's office with his claim to one of those small rooms . . . Stangeler sponged off with cold water and slipped into his uniform again. The soap smelled, he felt how his arms and shoulders seemed alive, how they breathed through the skin, felt heavy. He wants to sit down to his writing again, he'd like to pick it up where he'd stopped, without interruption, but that's totally impossible even though it would really be the right thing to do – there is always a long detour that he is annoyingly drawn into; only afterward does one gradually feel capable of the simplest little activities . . .

A soccer game or the war or Kerensky, or even Herr Hampe's constant chatter, and everything that's being read about in the newspapers out there – especially the war or the gigantic distance from here to Peking, for instance on the caravan route through the Gobi desert – "Rembrandt and a piece of wood" is a sentence in a book somewhere – and here is the little table. It is standing in front of the bed and he knows that since the detonation that knocked the breath out of him and is still reverberating off in the distance, tender springs are bubbling forth daily as if in answer, silver rippling out of the debris and rubble of what went before; but you can't simply jump from one to the other, can't let everything out there stand around disorganized and just count the little table in along with Peking and Kerensky, because it would just shrivel up next to them . . . That's the wrong mood, there's no fun in that, but often that's just the way it is. You ought to create order, bring the newspaper and the soccer game with you, all finished, and then – but how do you bring together, for example, the handsome Dorian Gray with Herr Fleischhanger or with me, the way we're locked away in the camp and get nothing but fish to eat – I'd like to see if someone like that would even be possible here – but, well, that's the war, a whirlwind, a whole mountain range of rubble and men that just goes on and on. In the end, you just squat there listlessly, everything's isolated, the broken shaft of a whip when I was four years old, then those incredibly Oriental horsemen at the railroad station in Manchuria and the door to the nursery, beside which the governess is washing; she's completely naked and therefore the door has to be closed – no, outside, another camp, you're torn away, carried off; yes, of course, crude methods, you end up invigorated or the other way, but it hasn't been carried to any sort of orderly conclusion inwardly, it just sort of hacks at you, so I can't get started on anything, there's no beam of light, no source, but to hell with it all, these eternal "latrines": – adieu!

Suddenly the silver springs are bubbling again, they're bubbling off to the side, in a closed room. Stangeler obeys willingly. Peking, Rembrandt, wood, the shaft of a whip, that all dries up quickly, then one has what one needs again, the silver stream that branches off – some sort of ground beneath one. You just have to deny those other things, they're simply outside – adieu!

Out of the haze and the shafts of light of a mass of time hardly accessible to the imagination, full of strange figures and candles and full of ponds of sadness and puddles of filth – from those masses back there glows, at first faintly, and then more distinctly, hovering closer and closer, the bright cell – quiet after the breathtaking detonation that split down to the ground, tore up, and brought to a halt that rockslide of emotional debris that rolled down from one generation to the next; and in answer, previously hidden springs bubbled out of the chasm – and at their origin, pressed together ardently, several of the young men (those who believed they were at a point of decision right then) sat in their cells here and there bent over a little seedling and hoped with trembling hearts to be able to nurse a "work" out of their flower pots (whose earth certainly did not yet reach back to the west). A new bubbling or blooming, fighting its way through the debris, branched off tenderly and full of denial from all that had gone before and avoided fearfully – yet at the same time with vitality and insight – those masses that had covered it previously and could still easily crush it. Things that had to be done, ought to be done, weighed heavily and as soon as one finally turned away from the broad, almost featureless current (how else than by turning away, really, could those who were so constituted make a start!?), one soon found oneself on narrow, steep paths, in constant anxiety; and the root of this torment gained strength daily. Because one ended up, as well, on strange, false tracks and with so much outward wandering around, one could end up on the course of those dull persisters who shrivelled up so repulsively when something new approached. Because what was new was feared – at first. Because one feared the crudeness of one's own masculine body, the joys of the soccer field – at first, because the foamed-up blood made itself known, coarsely, for long afterwards, the body swelled boastfully, the developing chest of the youth popped its seams in its lust for growth; indeed because everything from out there

– whichever of all those masses of flooding light struck or even found its way into the narrow tunnel of effort – actually caused alarm, since it so easily blocked or shadowed the still so narrow, restricted entrance. Strange things faced one: the performance of one's body, the life of man, the power of love – nothing from out there was anything other than an enemy, a disturbance, something that had to be overcome. One feared any sort of change at all, since one was a long way from getting all that had come pouring in up till now into some sort of order.

Yes, the young men of that sort feared the clumps of broken world, the debris, the fragments that came roaring in on them, they feared the dull blow that playfully destroys one not yet ripe. The silver springs of new life bubbled out of them after the thunder had subsided – it was as if clouds drifted up to the right and left of their youthful heads, their hearts swelled in reverence and astonishment, when they could see around some edge or little corner of the mass of debris more easily, no matter how little of it all could reach into their cells or how far they still were from being able to understand that it was blood of one blood, flesh of one flesh, fiber of one and the same muscle, the blow of one fist – all that seemed so disconcertingly and annoyingly separated, separated by such an airless gorge over which one had to jump, with such exertion, from the soccer field over there back here to concentration . . .

The light, the cell, the low house, with its drawn-out wings on a hill, the night, the cool, swaying, leafy cupola of endless forests; between these, which accompany it darkly on its banks, the mighty river surges northward, then turns, at its end, toward the rising sun and makes its way slowly, glittering and gray, into the sound between the seas of Japan and Okhotsk, opposite the northern tip of Sakhalin Island. The weak current stagnates a little against their waves. Where the river passes through inhabited land, it carries powerful steamers as large as ocean liners and grimy tugs. The city of Khabarovsk is loosely strewn out, temporary almost, like a camp; it is scarcely to be believed that someone could remember back to anything warm or tender there, like a certain corner of the garden in childhood – yet it happens! Many corrugated metal roofs are to be seen, shimmering on the edge of the city, whose barracks lose themselves in the wide, open country. In summer, the horizon often blazes up darkly in long strips. Indolently, licking its way forward almost unnoticeably, the fire progresses over the steppe; the fresh, coarse air becomes acrid and without a trace of its lovely, summery caress. The railroad trains are tiny against the landscape, then grow from small, red cubes to freight car after freight car, then out over the gigantic arches of the bridge that spans the river which is already like a lake there, but shortly beyond the bridge still takes in the Usuri. The waters stretch to the edge of sight and the shore already has sandy flats like the sea. The trains hurry off to the west, through changeless country, over changeless rails, through changeless forests, across the Urals, through small, provincial Russian towns with their boulevards, girls' schools, their reading clubs – secretly revolutionary – through changeless plains. Vassily caught sight of the neighbors' new servant girl for the first time as she bent over to tie up the beans, but by then she'd already been in town for three days; and later he could never forgive himself for those three days which he'd already spent in her proximity without knowing it, not even long after she'd become the wife he loved so much. Indeed, the way it happened was as if the whole, gloomy rockslide of emotion within him had been split down to the ground, torn up, brought to a stop; in response, hitherto concealed springs bubbled out of this chasm, fighting their way free of the debris, oh, and Vassily suddenly turned away, tenderly and shaking his head, from the entire previous, coarse life.

The land is friendly and the sunflowers gape mutely and peasant-pretty from the gardens along the corso, the "Bolshaya," the grandest street in town. – How else, other than branching off from the wide, almost featureless current of surrounding events, how else would these young people in the academies and universities and the forbidden clubs have been able, over the years, to begin and partially complete their repudiation of the status quo? The silver springs of new life, new future, went on bubbling out of them. The progressing events, however, had for years been pushing themselves together into a mountain range of rubble and human bodies; and the hopes for peace, awakened by the bourgeois revolution of 1917, turned back exhausted and transformed into bitterness from the wall that closed off the west, indeed separated all the countries of Europe from one another. February of 1917 saw the end of the czarist regime in Russia. This was an act of a bourgeoisie that had ripened to the point of taking over power. From the vantage point of the feudal state, one would not have been able to discern this very young, indeed almost unprecedented, Russian middle class during the war. Industry, transportation, provisioning – all this had been directed and accomplished by the bourgeoisie. The war was destined, so to speak, to bring home to that class its own importance, and in those bourgeois ranks were not just a few people who – even if they were still loyal to the idea of a "nation" – really regarded the entire current situation as a prime opportunity to put an end to the czarist regime, an opportunity that under no circumstances was to be missed. Rarely do historic events of epochal significance occur as smoothly as the fall of the Romanovs. One cannot imagine a better-ordered revolution; it snapped into place everywhere, from St. Petersburg to Vladivostok, like an oiled lock. The bourgeoisie assumed constitutionally the prerogatives that they had, in fact, had under the dissolute czarist state. That was all. Of course, arm in arm with the large, noble landowners. The Entente was assured of complete loyalty and devotion; the war was continued, of course. The army and the administration remained, on the whole, as they nad been. The president of the first "revolutionary" cabinet was a Prince Lvov and sitting at first in the most radical and revolutionary wing of that government was a lawyer named Kerensky, whose party color amounted to a thoroughly salon-worthy pale pink, all the more salon-worthy when ethical-social perfume somehow actually became high fashion.

Off to the side were things called workers' and soldiers' councils, the "St. Petersburg Soviet," which played at being the opposition, but was not about to pick up the hot potato and actually run the government. They preferred to leave that, as well as the responsibility, to others and limited themselves to criticizing. Meanwhile, Kerensky's career flourished, full of that "ill-defined striving to get ahead that forms the secret propellant of parliamentary life," as Oskar Blum says. Kerensky was, in turn Vice-Chairman of the Workers' and Soldiers' Council (an odd chairman for such a body), Minister of Justice, Minister of War, Commander-in-Chief of the Army, and finally, dictator. But not for long. It wasn't that he wasn't clever enough, but he just didn't have what it took to really pull it off. There was a lot of talk about the "people" throughout all of that revolution, but nobody really paid much attention to them. They existed for the most part in the form of an army of millions still in the trenches on the German front, and that army had already started to fall apart during the last days of the Czar. Now there were beginning to be shortages of necessary equipment.

Seldom does history stride across the threshold between one epoch and the following one without obvious catastrophe. Accordingly, here in Russia at the time, the actual transition was still to come. At the time there was a lot of talk of "democracy" in Russia. The war-weary army, the peasants, and the workers were promised peace; two days later the Entente was promised that Russia would hold out until the final victory. Land reform was discussed unendingly in "preliminary commissions" and the big land holders were reassured just as interminably of the inviolability of thier prerogatives. And so it was posssible, with time, to end up in the situation of a man who has one foot on the shore and the other on a ship that is in the act of casting off. For the moment, that departing ship was still connected to the shore by a gangway called "democracy and unity." Kerensky ran back and forth on this little gangway – there was nothing else for him to do, since he couldn't accomplish anything on either side – until one end slid off because of the ever-widening gap and he fell into the water.

On the evening of the third of April, 1917, Lenin arrived from Switzerland and climbed out at the Finland Station in St. Petersburg. Of course there was an official reception – Lenin was one of the "Men of 1905", even if one who, back then, conceived of the revolution in a certain unpleasant way, even today hardly imagined by the bourgeoisie. Chkheidze gave the following address: "Comrade Lenin. I welcome you to Russia in the name of the St. Petersburg Soviet, in the name of the revolution. But do not forget that it is our task to defend the revolution from internal as well as external attack. What we need is unity within democracy. We hope that you will pursue this common goal together with us."

There was silence. Lenin turned entirely around very slowly, so that he presented his back to Chkheidze. He was now directly facing the crowd of soldiers and workers who were mutely waiting. He filled his broad chest with air and spoke to them: "Worthy comrades, soldiers, sailors, and workers! I am happy to salute you as part of the victorious Russian revolution and as the vanguard of the army of the world proletariat. This predatory, imperialistic war is the beginning of civil war in all of Europe. The hour is approaching when our comrade Karl Liebknecht will give the sign for the people to turn their weapons against their exploiters, against the capitalists. The dawn of the socialist world revolution has come. In Germany, all is in a state of foment. Between today and tomorrow the entire structure of European imperialism may collapse. The Russian revolution, which you have brought about, has prepared the way for the catastrophe and begun a new epoch. Long live the socialist world revolution!"

This was spoken the way all speeches of that sort have to be – thrown together from ready-made phrases and slogans, but with clarity. A short time later, Lenin had to go into hiding in the Petersburg workers' quarter, while his comrade Leo Trotsky was already under lock and key.

Little happened until fall, and what did was merely an expression of indecision and a situation that could only breed discord. The thirtieth of April bore the monstrosity of a coalition cabinet between the "Social Revolutionaries" – as the bourgeois groups were still calling themselves – and the Communists. The spring also brought Kerensky's gamble on an offensive ordered over the protests of the general staff, even though the army was no longer in condition to be sent into battle. And indeed, the attack ended in a miserable debacle. Kerensky apparently wanted to follow the example of the French Revolution – totally invalid here – of suppressing internal problems by means of a victorious campaign against the external enemy – a vain daydreamer's disregard for the facts. The third of July saw a Bolshevik revolt in St. Petersburg as a result, so to speak, of the abortive, lunatic offensive. The twenty-seventh of August brought, as a reaction, Kornilov's rightist putsch. Nothing decisive in any of that. What was decisive was that Lenin was there, that someone there had the courage to confront the whole situation, the courage to completely destroy all that had gone before, to tear apart all the patchwork, to embrace chaos. The pendulum had to swing far to the other side, indeed, so far that one could seriously consider that in some hitherto unknown way it was going to remain hanging over there at the extreme of its swing and never return.

In the night of the twenty fifth of October, the Winter Palace in St. Petersburg was stormed. Kerensky escaped. It can be said with complete certainty that he would literally have been torn to pieces if the mob had gotten hold of him. From Gatchina he made one last attempt to assert his power. The sailors of the Baltic Fleet destroyed it forever. That was the victory of the communist, or as they also say, "Bolshevik" revolution. The red flag soon waved from west to east, from Petersburg to Vladivostok. To add to that – despite the official peace treaty finally concluded with Germany at Brest-Litovsk in the spring of 1918 – this all-consuming alternative to the hopelessly complicated forms of life and economy in the west rose up like a wall of flames separating the Soviet Empire from Europe, thus protecting the first impulses of a new Russian age – flowing away from the current of what had gone before like a silvery, bubbling rivulet – from the destructive germs of western rootlessness and, above all, from short-sighted, petty criticism. Even German talent as well as Jewish resourcefulness were at first denied commercial access because of uncertainty about private property; in other words, they could not (similar to the way they did at home during the war) piss on the cornerstone of the growing edifice of destiny, they could not promptly turn the ponderous struggles of Russia into personal gain, and they could not – behind the scenes – issue shares for the commercial by-products of world history with the excuse of extreme economic hardship; on the contrary, hunger and want raged unchecked, as fate would have it. The red flag waved from west to east, from Petersburg to Vladivostok.

In the summer of 1918, however, the gigantic body of Red Russia, stretched out toward the east, was cut in two as if by the slash of a saber – just politically, of course, in the sense of political power. Bad luck would have it that the well equipped and armed military transport units of the Czech Legion, that army group formed in Russia in the fall of 1914 from Austrian deserters – similar to the Serbian-South Slavic "Druzhina" and more or less to the Polish Legion, in which, however, there were also ethnic Russians from Poland – bad luck would have it, then, that these Czech transport units were distributed all along the huge, long railroad line from Europe to the east; the Red government had halted them because they had not fulfilled the condition by which – after the peace of Brest-Litovsk and the dissolution of the German front, on which they had fought – they had been allowed to use the railroad to proceed to Vladivostok in order to board ship for France, where they would be sent to the western front; the Czechs had refused, namely, to lay down their arms. In fact, their evacuation was not the uppermost on their minds. These men, whose situation was tenuous, were being used by the reactionary groups in the eastern Russian and Siberian cities – the "Whites" – to suddenly grab power by means of a putsch along the entire, long stretch of rails from Vladivostok to the Volga; and it worked. In eastern Russia, they occupied Kasan, Simbirsk, Samara, and other cities. With a single stroke, they had control of the railroad, the only lifeline from west to east, and that meant, at least in Siberia, having absolute power. Now, in other words, that Czech insect that had been sitting completely still – encapsulated so to speak, during all the early days of the Bolshevik revolution – now it was sitting on the skin of part of the nation like a bloodthirsty tick, eating and drinking its fill. The Siberian reactionaries had made use of the Czechs; in fact their entire success depended on them, at least in the beginning. It was the extraordinary fighting power of these mercenaries alone that held back the Red assault that came immediately from western Russia; this new "White" Siberian state under the presidium of the "Regent" Kolchak still extended far beyond the Urals and into Europe. And in the subsequent period, one enemy after the other rose up against Red Russia, not the least of which were hunger and typhus and the already mentioned lack of the things of civilization – clothing, weapons, shoes, and medicines. Beyond the borders however, it now appeared that the whole world had designs on the motherland: the hungry Germans plundered the land in the west, despite the peace treaty. Generals and Cossack leaders like Iudenich, Denikin, Dutov, Anenkov and others fought against the Red state with sizable armies. The English occupied the Kola Peninsula, were pushing down from the north and as well from the direction of Jamburg toward St. Petersburg. And into Siberia – just as they did later, in 1920, into South Russia and Poland – the Entente sent their support troops and military missions. English and American soldiers, strong boned and well nourished, lounged around the railroad stations in the east and observed, contemptuously spitting tobacco juice, the Russian formations that Kolchak had organized to fight the Reds by pointing machine guns at them and exercising them to the point of collapse to make them obedient. In the towns, French officers bought women and the butter that had become scarcer and scarcer and English lieutenants bargained skillfully with their half-starved and frozen Austrian counterparts and bought cheaply their solid gold medals for bravery in the face of the enemy – as mementos, they said. However, the most important thing the Entente brought was not the few boys in the west, east, and south – certainly not a decisive contribution to Kolchak when compared to his Russian troops as well as the 30,000 Czech, 15,000 Polish and South Slavic Legionnaires – but rather the money, the artillery, the munitions, the tanks, the vehicles, the canned food, the shoes, the uniforms. Out there in the east, almost without a sound, the Japanese had entered the country; and in the harbors of Vladivostok, the English and American battleships rode at anchor, emitting thick smoke from behind their armor plate. That's how things stood for Red Russia – indeed, it can be said that things weren't really standing at all, that the nation was going over the edge of the thundering cataract of its fate and no one could see anything but the end – the horizon was on fire.

But by December 30, 1920, the Eighth Soviet All-Russian Congress was already issuing the demobilization orders signed by Kalinin. Every opponent had been beaten.

Does anyone grasp the secret of that empire? Yes, of course, one can offer explanations and reasons, one can talk about the Bolshevik agitators who managed to win over the enemy soldiers to their cause, or the many peasant revolts incited to help the Reds, and resulting skirmishes that hurt the Whites at every step; or one can even point to the dominating personality of Lenin or to Leo Trotsky's military genius. In the end, one might even offer the war-weariness of the Entente states as an explanation or even adduce the parliamentary difficulties which arose in those countries when the left wing parties raised objections to the appropriation of the necessary funds for the intervention in Russia.

Is the victory of the bitterest poverty and want over the power of riches thereby explained, the victory of a single, simplistic concept over the far-seeing worldly wisdom of the West; does all of that explain a victory achieved contrary to every reasonable expectation – one that prevented, once and for all, Russia's becoming a province and offshoot of the West?

Does anyone grasp the secret of this empire? What does it mean that the Reds triumphed despite every reasonable expectation and chased the foreigners out of their country, what does it mean that this communism, which is of highly western intellectual heritage, in the end fulfilled the task of closing Russia off from the West for the longest time; and what does it mean, finally, that the much-announced "World Revolution," on which the entire communist idea depends in the last analysis – this end stage of the "Dictatorship of the Proletariat" – never occurred? Was Lenin, the internationalist, freethinker, and atheist perhaps just the most faithful servant of Holy Russia, so loyal that he himself was unable to realize it, something that would become clear only at a later date???

Billowing fog hid completely from those leaders, who had to act forcefully, the image of a distant future, the sight of which might have entirely robbed them of their conviction; yet all those convictions were precisely the best means of serving it. But now, in the bright present, the unlikeliest thing imaginable was the first to occur: by the spring of 1919 the front was beginning to push its way further and further toward Siberia, from west toward east – a dark mountain range of rubble, flames, and human bodies that extended forward into the immeasurable breadth of the country.

Now, and in the bright present, that most improbable thing also appeared in its individual details and affected individual people, and things that were widely separated often came together in mind-boggling confrontations. Since life itself began to evolve more and more in the form of a dream, it was even possible, for instance, that a salesman from a large Viennese fashion house, Hugo Blau, who had come to Siberia as a war prisoner, suddenly began to play a role there in the Red Guard, indeed, even more – that he eventually became the dangerous adversary of a man who certainly never would have dreamed that such a thing was possible . . . Blau did not, as a matter of fact, use his real name when he joined the Red Guard in Barna-Ul after the October Revolution in 1917, but appropriated a Czech name instead, almost as if he had predicted that he'd end up a prisoner of the Whites, at which point such a name might well be of help to him. And so, in the summer of 1918 after the Czech putsch, when he was locked up in Novo-Nikolaevsk along with other members of the Red Guard, he skillfully played the role of the Czech sympathizer who'd only joined the Red Guard under duress. And Blau suppported his efforts very effectively with a large number of denunciations, by means of which he delivered to the Whites' knives a long list of people in the city who'd sympathized with the Reds, as well as former comrades who'd gone into hiding. In that way Blau – or Nadvoniek as he now called himself – managed to work himself into a position where he no longer risked sharing the gruesome fate of his former Red "comrades," but soon was actually the most important man in the so-called "Investigative Department." Numerous Bolsheviks came before the firing squad simply through his efforts. Blau also soon proved that it was dangerous to oppose him. This was learned, in particular by a captain of the reserves – then commandant of the prisoner-of-war camp situated high above the city of Novo-Nikolaevsk – who got involved in things that were not within his jurisdiction. This captain – who was, in fact, very popular among the Germans and Austrians in his charge because of his kindness and consideration – tried to influence the White officers to treat the Red Guard prisoners in the municipal jail more humanely; he even opposed the continuing investigations, patrols, and house-to-house searches in the town, on the reasonable grounds that all of that was hardly likely to make the new White regime popular and that peoples' nerves needed to be calmed. And in fact, milder methods were introduced. With all those activities, however, the captain soon found himself at cross purposes with one Hugo Blau, alias Nadvoniek, because the latter had good reason to carry on more fanatically that any White terrorist. Blau began a regular campaign of defamation and soon got results, since it was waged cleverly and on several fronts simultaneously. It suddenly appeared that the captain's attitude was clearly no longer quite dependable, his friendly relationships with the captured officers up there in the camp were held against him, and other things besides – in short, his position in Novo-Nikolaevsk gradually become very unpleasant, since the attack on him was joined by all those people whose cruelty and baseness he'd tried to oppose. The captain lost his patience, had himself transferred, and eventually assumed command of a unit on the Volga front. Blau, however, who perhaps sensed that he had really carried things too far, disappeared forever not long afterward – no one knew where. History as it evolved was simply so abruptly changeable and, as it were, so faithless to anyone who set his heart on it, that one did not have to be a fully developed scoundrel to end up changing colors and sides – all it took was barely viable seeds of human baseness and soon they were growing as if they were in a greenhouse. One has merely to realize that there were no less than four sequential political upheavals in Siberia, namely: the fall of czarism at the hands of the bourgeoisie in February and March of 1917, then the fall of this bourgeois regime through the actions of the communists in October 1917; then in the summer of 1918 the Whites took power there, only to be destroyed forever by Red troops in the beginning of 1920.

Out of the haze and shafts of light from a mass of departed time, long since inaccessible to the imagination, full of strange figures and candles – from those masses back there glows, at first faintly, and – there! – more distinctly, hovering nearer, that bright cell in the quiet interval before and after all those breathtaking detonations that split apart, tore up, and brought to a halt those rockslides of spirit and tradition that rolled down from one generation to the next. Every which way, pushing and rebounding, here within, there outside, previously hidden torrents roared out of the chasms. But for the moment, in 1918 and 1919, at least, men were still sitting in the prison camps here and there – even if those well-maintained islands (tennis court, garden, casino) had already begun to erode in the course of history, befouled here and there by the fight for existence that had once again become necessary.

The talented ones made workshops out of their quiet cells and beside many a bed stood a workbench or a printing press and on the bed lay the necessary raw materials, scrounged up in the city with a good deal of running around in the bitter cold. The untalented ones, however, limped along and joined in, offended – a repulsive sight. They were like worms that go wriggling away when a rotten fence post that's been lying around somewhere is lifted up to make room for a new one. There were already deep splits here and there in that self-contained state within a state and with the wind that blew through the holes that had developed in the plank fence – stolen and burned – came a cloud of seeds of new possibilities and opportunities, by means of which some found the right track and finally made their way out of the camp and back to their individual lives. If one had often thoroughly annoyed oneself and others during the close coexistence there, inside, those fine, hairsplitting differences paled now in comparison with the oppressively simple and crude parting of the ways outside, namely: Red or White? Under the Red regime, following the "peace" with Germany, the eastern camps had started to empty out, the men transferred west to be exchanged; going home by sea was simply not a possibility for such large numbers at that point. Now everything was turned around. Many of those desperate men whose march home was cut off in 1918 by the gulf which had formed between Red Russia and White Siberia were now dragged back into Siberia, and then eventually even further back, during the retreat before the wall of flames advancing from the Red Front toward the west. Because, as was known from experience, the Bolshevik agitators always did their best to recruit those battle-tested soldiers and no one wanted to let priceless human material fall into the hands of the advancing enemy and thus strengthen him. In this way, the Siberian camps came to be abandoned or combined over and over again.

At nightfall, extending from the brick buildings and plank fences out beyond the dirty slush and out into the gloomy distance where the snow can be presumed to be cleaner and where the great cold starts, a new column of men from a western internment camp comes stumbling and staggering along, with rucksacks and clanking tea-pots, into the still more or less fenced-in, broad rectangle of the Krasnoyarsk camp. The following day Stangeler went looking for Snobby; he knew he was there somewhere. With luck, he soon found him and it was Snobby, the one and only Snobby, who'd also had to give up his former independent ways; but one could tell that all this was just a passing phase. Snobby appeared to have lost neither his previous inclination for elegant modulation of voice and movement of hand, nor to have given up, even here, all his clever little tricks, as Stangeler soon realized with great admiration. He'd hardly known Snobby earlier – he was big for his age – had only seen him at his parents' house. But that such an article, such a name, was there, that was reason enough for looking him up without further consideration. Then Dorian came, the friend with whom Snobby lived, and one could tell by looking at this Dorian that he was not entirely happy with things, the way he acted like an uninvolved bystander, no matter what their conversation touched upon. The way Snobby told it, he wasn't a bystander at all, Snobby said he was doing some writing and that he also painted . . . Stangeler followed Snobby's outstretched hand with his eyes and saw two oil paintings and got mad, thinking of his eldest sister who'd always had artistic pretensions. Talking with Snobby, Stangeler immediately adopted, dutifully and not without effort, a tone which still pretty well reflected his earlier behavior, even though that had since been altered or completely abandoned, and so he got along quite well with Snobby; the latter didn't need to be make an effort – Snobby was nothing more than a tall, healthy boy, an English-German halfbreed.

The new arrivals were delighted with the spaciousness which the camp offered. The severe winter limited life, to be sure, to the brightness and warmth of the quarters, but even there one was not squeezed into a corner (ten or fifteen officers or so lived in one room) and eventually one learned what the place had to offer – plenty, obviously, since there were 8,000 inmates, officers and men: six coffee houses, in some respects quite comfortable, a theater, libraries. Certain men were most impressed by a small, round clock tower, a kind of kiosk in the very center of the camp, in the "city," so to speak; there all the announcements from the administration were posted. The landscape, its enormity hidden for the most part behind snow squalls, became, on the occasional clear winter days, astonishingly visible, glittering off into the distance – the camp was situated above the city. Generally, though, one could appreciate the total picture only through its parts or fragments – this collision of the mighty, heaved-up, forested mountain range from the south with the steppe that hastened off to the north in grayish, snowy mist; and in between lay, rigid and dull white, the meandering ribbon of the Yenesei. There were now roads leading over the frozen river, across which scurried miniature horse-drawn sleds. One could comprehend this scarcely comprehensible massiveness and what it held only in the extreme fragments and pieces, and, so to speak, only out of the corner of the eye, as the tears started to run together in the grim cold – and so one made the daily rounds of the broad parade ground, self-imposed for the sake of health, walking rapidly and counting every circuit, because the winter, with its forty degrees below zero, had already penetrated, no matter how thickly one was bundled up – only the minority possessed fur coats.

The arrival of the newcomers brought about many a reacquaintance. Johann von Valoisky had come across two school friends, the brothers Ernst and Egon von Ress; Lieutenant Jan Alwersik had met up with a friend and colleague from his regiment, First Lieutenant Josip Hitschka. And so, all three, Alwersik, Stangeler, and Valoisky – they'd also stuck together during the journey out there – had found their ways into separate groups of friends in the gigantic camp; but eventually, these groups soon came into contact and mixed together again.

Dorian and Stangeler, the two Gymnasium students (in reality they weren't much more) stuck together. At the Café Intime, they made the first attempts to feel out each other's philosophy with regard to basic literature. Afterward Stangeler even managed to pry manuscripts out of Dorian – at first without having to turn over any of his own, that was just the way he was – then he clutched his booty under his fur coat, hurried away to his quarters – which he shared with fourteen Turkish officers – and spread the pages out on his improvised little wooden table, his heart pounding all the while. Then a stone came loose from that serious heart and went rolling downhill -there were actually some pretty tolerable lines of prose and even several poems which were enjoyable, even if incomparably stranger and more tender than anything that Stangeler had been able to get from Ernst von Ress up till then.

That camp, like every one, contained many poets.

That camp, just like any other one at the time, also contained and supported many workshops, businesses and stores, with all the necessary connections to the city. A steady stream of prisoners with permits passed in and out through the gate. Sleds came in loaded with raw materials, sleds went back out loaded with splendidly labelled bottles of miserable liqueur, or full of elegantly finished overshoes for women, or mouthwash. There was hardly a trademark from back home that was spared from misappropriation and the print shops in the camp had their hands full turning out labels in color. There were even companies that issued stock, such as the dyeworks that had been set up in an empty barracks. What many had correctly predicted, during the period of waiting when time had been forced to stop, had occurred some time ago and there was once again opportunity for activity. Even the separation between the officers' camp and that of the enlisted men had almost completely disappeared, the plank fence dividing them having been stolen and burned, and what resulted was a fruitful exchange between intelligence and rough strength.

For several weeks, even Alwersik had been going in and out through the gate more frequently, without business-related reasons, of course.

The student Stangeler lay on his bunk, the other sat next to him. When Stangeler shut his eyes, he saw Dorian's face close before him, that countenance hovering close, the single person, the other one, to whom he felt attracted day and night, whose absence elicited a fine torment, by which everything around him was animated.

Alwersik was sitting down below in the city with Katia Poccal, the wife of a Polish captain who was fighting the Reds at the front far to the west. The tiny living room in the little house was toasty warm. So, something had turned up there after all and he saw nothing the least astonishing about that and stood and sat and lay around there, just as relaxed yet ready to move on as had always been the case with him, despite all of his impetuousness. She speaks German, that's comforting, once she was even an Austrian, that's the best part of it, even if she really became a Russian long ago – several years before, she'd married the Russian-Polish landowner Poccal, and besides that, she even had Slavic blood from her mother's side. And now she'd landed in that Siberian garrison town and was sitting there in front of Alwersik, with a full throat white as milk and distracted dark eyes that seldom revealed anything and with full breasts and small hands and feet.

What with all that, the social circles had begun to mix. Already Ernst von Ress, whom everyone quickly came to like, was talking more frequently with Josip Hitschka, who was inclined to think systematically, out loud, and impulsively; already Snobby and Valoisky, the one too tall, the other too short, were taking their turns around the parade ground together; Stangeler was already discussing possible warm weather sports activities with Snobby's friends; even Alwersik had rather taken a liking for the tall, much-traveled Snobby. Dorian, however, he only met thanks to a comradely treat with Turkish coffee and pastries that took place in Stangeler's room.

Almost immediately afterward there was a kind of collision between Jan Alwersik and Stangeler, a collision that occurred almost without words or looks. What Alwersik said was: "Dorian, er, Snobby (he gave a little snort through his nose while pronouncing the name), well, Dorian, that's . . ." What remained unspoken was, "I'm not going to come to blows with you over it, my dear Stangeler, I'll just have to put up with it, but it looks like I have my work cut out for me here . . ." The student, however, became evasive (almost surprisingly), withdrew, seemed to be bothered by something from another quarter – he shook his head slowly, looked up and directly into Alwersik's eyes. To both of them, the face of the other, directly opposite, seemed very close and familiar and yet, at the same time, to a certain extent, was standing there free and alone, solitary and self-contained, the way a tree or rock in the landscape opposes itself to man. Anyway, they shook hands.

Alwersik was lying next to Katia in the warm, half-darkened, quiet room. Her left breast filled his hand. The woman lay against him like a soft cloud, merging dimly with the boundary where purple solitude began indistinctly – he could not tell clearly where that was – but from there it went inward, deeper within himself. He felt her breast lying in his hand, the hand held, hefted, possessed. He swam as if in quiet waters with this, his milky, sweet mother, with the sweet inclination of her head, with the many charming faces that snuggled against him, as if they had climbed out of his own purple. A subtle annoyance grated against this quiet, the subtle annoyance that Dorian's solitary behavior had been causing him for several days: the boy had really lost his head over that Snobby.

Separated from Snobby, however, Dorian was not irritable or alienated from himself or others: his eyes opened more widely, his features actually softened somewhat, even his hair was less stiff, and he didn't just talk, he actually said something on occasion. Stangeler listened delightedly and, at the same time, in hopes of profiting. They had just come in out of the glaring winter sun and into the dark stairwell of the barracks where Stangeler lived in a room with fourteen Turkish officers. The room was quite large and bright and from its three windows one could see quite a distance, as far as the city down below, with its many, small details. Dorian sat down on Stangeler's bed. Next door, behind the wall, footsteps were going back and forth – "More Turks," said Stangeler. "More Turks," thought Dorian absent-mindedly in response, and then started to speak suddenly. Dorian told about a girl (her name was Katharina) in a bright, upstairs room, saying that he used to wait for her there, and he became so tender that Stangeler tried hard, in hopes of profiting, to follow it all perfectly, for God's sake, and of course he imagined a girl with legs, standing on a floor in a room in an apartment in a building on a street just as little as Dorian did – what they both were actually doing was using light and colors as building materials and passing through parts of the city that, in reality, didn't even exist at home in Vienna.

In the midst of all that, the countryside roundabout was beginning to arise from the oppressiveness and storms of the winter. Just as, by the light of the rising moon, the hills and forests open their eyes and gaze directly at man, so now, on milder and windless days, the landscape lay placidly spread out before the unaccustomed beholder – steppe and river and the sky arching over to the forested mountains. No longer did the cold bite into one's eyes. It seemed balmy, even if the thermometer still showed eight degrees below zero.

Alwersik soon felt more confident. He spent his days almost exclusively with Dorian. They were often a pair now, and even if not always, more distinctly each time. His powers of observation were constantly in sharp focus and he began to develop the ability to dissect and interpret the most trivial events – something that had been totally foreign to him up till then. He thought consistently and firmly, and in that connection he talked a lot with Josip Hitschka again – however, never about the things that really mattered to him. These he considered in a logical fashion together with Stangeler; the Gymnasium student participated eagerly.

Because Alwersik and he had agreed early on; and at the same time it was recognized as a basic fact – and was thus formulated by the student as well – that only those things could be permitted to happen that "would contribute to Dorian's further development and to the clearing away of debris" – that's how the slant-eyed scholar and skilled soccer player put it as he walked away with both hands full of material to be organized, and disappeared, not without a few heartaches, behind the heroic subterfuge that, in this case, Alwersik was exactly right. Stangeler was very preoccupied – with himself, of course.

Beyond that Alwersik invited the student – but not Dorian, however – to a small banquet, which took place in the room where he lived with Hitschka and a third comrade. It was an epicurean feast in the extreme: a hearty bouillon, wiener schnitzel – all from the sixtieth dog caught and slaughtered. Afterward, ample coffee. The third roommate, a first lieutenant, a quiet and brave man – it was actually he who'd caught and splendidly prepared number sixty and smoked the remainder for later use – scarcely said a word during the meal or afterward, didn't really even bother to join in, because what Hitschka, Alwersik, and Stangeler accomplished in that respect exceeded even their gluttony. During coffee, when mouths were no longer full, there was a decisive shift to metaphysics and theology. Josip's eyes glowed; at times, he was totally distracted by his efforts to think, his gaze directed at the ceiling. It was a quite a while later that the men finally thought about going to bed. The scholar went back to his quarters delighted and enlightened.

And so they soon turned completely away from the landscape that lay there foreign and cold and inaccessible because of the snowdrifts; they turned completely toward the illuminated, accessible, hospitable interior. The clique at the Café Intim had gotten to be quite sizable; only Snobby's friends were gradually pushed to the side, brought to dead silence by the way people debated there, that is, by Hitschka, Dorian, Alwersik, Stangeler, actually even Snobby in the end (he was pulled in) and Valoisky, the latter with especially aggressive enthusiasm. During one conversation about faith and the power of the will, Valoisky insisted rigidly that these strengths deserved the highest respect, in and of themselves, regardless of the object to which they were directed. For instance, he said, if someone were to spend his whole life heroically claiming he had a glass belly and had to put up with ridicule, scorn, and the looney bin because of it – "well, hats off to such a man!!!" he yelled with a voice that cracked and stood up, feigning a salute. On the very next day, a caricature made the rounds, showing Valoisky – the resemblance was a scream – saluting the glass belly. The perpetrator was Alwersik.

Throughout the years passed in one camp or another, the countryside, extending far and wide on all sides, remained constant and with it, the peasants for whom war and upheaval passed by as distant events. With its onion domes, the village lies amidst midday sun and the dying peal of bells, swimming like a cork on the gigantic undulating waves of rock and forest that wander off into sunlit distance and passing time.

Once again, summer had come, once again the medical corpsman Alois Dvorak and the infantryman Kajetan Uiberbacher (a mountain guide by profession back home) decided to break out. They were interned in the camp at Saratov, in European Russia. The guards back in those days, 1917, were still quite strict. At one point in the high plank fence there was a small, barred doorway for removing garbage. Alois and Kajetan wanted to be on their way as night fell. There were four men from Salzburg in the camp, good singers. Whenever they started up together, the Russians completely forgot about their guard duty. They came from all sides, from every post, stood in a circle leaning on their rifles and listened with eyes welling over or with a shock of blond hair protruding from under their caps and hanging down over their foreheads. Yodeling was particularly admired and received generous applause. Meanwhile Kajetan was taking the door off its hinges so that it was only held by the lock, but this was hardly noticeable. During the night they slipped away. There was a curious quality to this wandering off with Kajetan – his instinct was as sure as that of an animal, his sense of direction almost miraculous, his eye as sharp as that of an eagle or buzzard. He tramped along comfortably beside the clumsy Dvorak, with a narrow-based stride that would be more at home on a steep path over mountain a ridge or on ice than here in this broad expanse, empty as far as the eye could see. One time, Dvorak argued with Kajetan about which path to take. The former believed himself absolutely right, but Kajetan prevailed; and in the end it turned out that his way was shorter and easier. After that, Dvorak trusted the Tyrolean blindly in such matters. They were headed toward a German colony, one of the many villages to be found in Russia that were made up totally of German immigrants. They intended to live and work there. In camp, all they got to eat was rotten fish, the beds were nothing but bare wood, there was no such thing as a Sunday or a holiday, just eleven hours spent pounding away at rocks, day in, day out.

Nourishment was provided along the way by the Russian peasant, who never had to be asked twice: milk, butter, cottage cheese, bread. The peasant put his dumb questions to the foreigners as they partook of his hospitality – they had to be far more intelligent, that was certainly clear to every Grigor or Nikolai. Uiberbacher looked into their dairy practices here and there and once he even managed to cure a sick cow. Great honor was heaped upon the foreigners; it became common knowledge that each of these Germans was a very clever man, if not actually a learned man, the latter finally proving to be the case when Dvorak extracted stone slivers from the wound of a boy who'd fallen, washed and bandaged him.

In this way they eventually arrived at the German colony, found welcoming words and plenty of work to do, and lived there for months with the Mecklenburgers. On one of the farms there were already three prisoners who'd made a good reputation for themselves, one named Busatti from the Italian Tyrol, and two sergeants from Brandenburg. However, none of them had been reported to the authorities, because the Germans were afraid that these able, valuable workers would be taken away from them again, since that had already happened once. So, if it came to that, they could hide five men.

On Sunday morning, each of them was handed a thick prayer book and sat in the Protestant village church, singing right along during the hymns – even the Catholic Austrians. Uiberbacher's beautiful singing voice made a favorable impression. Afterwards they enjoyed a stroll, at leisure and neatly dressed as they now were, through the sunny village, along the neat main street with its row of poplars and tile roofs. There on the Russian plain, the German village, widely known for its "being different" and its tidy roofs, seemed so exotic and reminiscent of home.

Yes, one turned his hat in his hand and even chatted with the girls, of course. Uiberbacher had things easy and hard. On one hand his singing, yodeling, and guitar playing were admired and brought him all sorts of invitations, but on the other hand, his dialect was absolutely the worst, so that he ended up using Russian to help him out in conversations with the young women. The clever and witty Dvorak had it easy, but, then, he also happened to be good-looking. The place was indebted to him for a completely new form of entertainment, namely the theater. He got together a troop and on Sundays they put on farces or "scenes from life" and things of the sort, but a lot of sentimental things as well. The success was incredible. There was a point in all this, however, because Uiberbacher's strumming and Dvorak's clever characters were both directed, when all was said and done, at a girl named Marfa. Things began to take on a certain watchful tension between the two men. Each one believed he was about to win out, though the Tyrolean may have been deceiving himself a bit. Because Dvorak had just about achieved success, it seemed to him, and Uiberbacher's slow ways probably only served to amuse Marfa – but on the other hand, how could you be so sure?

Just then, however, this peaceful existence was abruptly terminated – all five men were arrested while at work out in the fields and put in jail in the nearest town, although they'd been promised – and the farmers as well – that they would just be taken back to the camp. So there they were, all five of them to one bunk. The farmers had been advised to proceed through the officially prescribed channels with their application to have the five men turned over to them legally and the Mecklenburgers had decided to do that, knowing full well that these "official channels" would be very expensive; otherwise, things would drag on forever. Now, however, they didn't even know that their five men were sitting there in jail; they thought they were already in the nearest prison camp. But when, one day, rumor had it that they were to be transferred from there directly to someplace far to the north – to a railroad construction crew where workers were badly needed – from then on the runaways had but one single thought: to get in touch with their employers some way or other.

At the moment, the holidays were being celebrated and the jail was packed with stone drunk Russians, civilian and military; the whole place had been puked all over and the stench was revolting. The five planned as follows: they would draw lots to see who would announce through the peephole in the cell door that he had to go to the latrine, where the wall was made of thin boards with loose nails. From there he would just slip away; with all the yelling and carrying on, his failure to return would certainly not be noticed. For the head count at ten o'clock at night, they intended to make a dummy out of rucksacks and blankets in one corner of the bunk. Busatti was picked and disappeared. Everything worked, even at roll call. The night was horrible. Fourteen totally plastered men were brought in, several bellowing like steers. They all threw up in the bucket standing in the corner, but it was already full to the brim.

One of them got mad at the guards for some reason or other, dragged the bucket over to the door, climbed up on it with astonishing care and confidence, and managed to piss through the barred opening and all over the soldiers sitting over their chess game outside. There was an uproar, someone banged on the door with a rifle butt, the pisser lost his balance and fell, upsetting the bucket with its sour, evil contents, which went sloshing off in every direction. The stench increased, insofar as that was possible. Our four men had lain down together at the end of the bunk, next to the bogus sleeper. Not until two o'clock did it become quiet; they were all trumpeting and sawing away in their sleep, except the four who were wide awake, waiting for Busatti. He would have needed around six hours to get out and back from the German colony; Busatti had taken off at nine in the evening and accordingly could be expected back at three. But he didn't show up. From Uiberbacher's corner remarks like "dirty wop" could already be heard. The Tyrolean smelled treason, that Busatti would simply stay out there without worrying about them. But at three thirty in the morning the guard brought Busatti in. The shift had just changed and their messenger had been smart enough to climb back into the latrine, fasten the loose board again, and wait until the new guard came on duty, so it would look like he'd been led out by the previous guard. The report: the villagers now knew what was going on and would do everything possible.

Not long after that, however, the five prisoners were actually taken to the nearest camp, some eighty versts away, and immediately put to work building a public garden in the city, where they were so ill-humored that all they did was to make a nuisance of themselves by tearing out or ruining more than they planted. When time began to draw on, they once again got the idea of trying something on their own. Dvorak and Uiberbacher kept an eye on each other, not because they had any idea of escaping together again; it was far more likely that each one of them was trying to figure out who would be the first to end up at Marfa's house and win the prize. One day as they were working in the park, a storm came up suddenly, something that happens on the plains. In the twinkling of an eye there was nothing but thunder and lightning and hailstones the size of eggs. The hail was so bad that all anyone wanted to do was find shelter somewhere; they all went running into the nearest buildings, prisoners and guards alike. During that very storm, however, Uiberbacher disappeared and never returned. Dvorak knew what that meant and resolved to take off right away, regardless of the danger – it didn't matter whether they shot at him. The efforts of the Mecklenburgers had been without success up to that point. Dvorak simply got up on his hind legs, as they say, and ran. It was quite clear to him that he was not likely to catch up to Uiberbacher, who had two days' head start, unless the Tyrolean had some reason for stopping along the way. And that's just what providence had in mind. Uiberbacher turned up at one of the villages he had to pass through just as the hog slaughter was starting. To his astonishment and chauvinistic contempt he discovered that they didn't seem to understand how to make sausage there, indeed had never even heard of it. Blood, liver, and all the rest were simply going to be thrown away unused?? He made himself a clean board, washed his hands, rolled his sleeves up to his armpits, and began his praiseworthy labors. By evening, the first blood pudding, bratwurst, and liverwurst was arriving on the table. The result was such that it could easily have been termed a turning point in the history of that village; actually they were not far from bestowing almost religious veneration on Uiberbacher. He then proceeded to similarly transform the referred-to parts of not less than five hogs and afterward taught his art to the peasants. This professorship, however, took up ten days, during which the Tyrolean ate his fill, because he'd been starving to death. Uiberbacher stuffed himself and the tenderest longings of his soul were in this fashion transiently put to sleep.

In the meantime, Dvorak had long since arrived at the hoped-for goal. Peaceful and satisfied in every respect, he was sitting on the veranda of one of the farmhouses at the edge of the village on a Sunday evening. The horizon was aglow, deep red, and the chirping of the crickets could be heard. Along the row of houses came a stocky figure, whose gait seemed somehow foreign. They called to Uiberbacher. He walked over to the railing, hardly returned their greeting. His bright, sharp eyes rested searchingly on Dvorak for the longest time. Finally he adjusted his rucksack, shoved his pipe over to the other corner of his mouth and said, "Dja know wot, Louie, I'd a never tho't ya'd do that."

Said it, turned, walked away with his narrow-gauge stride, and was not to be enticed back. For the longest time he could be seen out there, marching off into the distance as the evening light gradually disappeared. He stayed in a German village about twenty versts away, but never again visited the place where he had previously worked.

Not long afterward, the Bolshevik revolution occurred and the war prisoners became so-called "free men" and could remain at their jobs without interference and live wherever they chose. After the Treaty of Brest-Litovsk in the spring of 1918, both Dvorak and Uiberbacher were exchanged and, after a difficult journey, arrived home. Because they had found themselves in a district not immediately affected by the Kolchak revolt.

Whenever Alwersik lay there with Katia, he would talk to her for hours without interruption, in a half-whisper. He would never have been able to say exactly what he had talked to her about, what she'd said or he'd said, or what the topic of conversation had been at any one time. It was just that the warm, hurried murmuring and whispering was so sweet and her soft, colorless, slightly whiny tone – the accent of her German wasn't Austrian and wasn't Russian, if anything more like the latter. For Alwersik it was her voice, the voice of his milky, sweet mother, with whom he chatted along happily. She always said whatever came to mind, often talked about her longing and remorse for her husband at the horrible front and she seemed to have a sort of childish and – so it seemed despite all – very deeply seated relationship with him; she frequently called Koloman Poccal "my good, ample mother." She also spoke of a brother, had no siblings otherwise, and about her great unhappiness and about a young man whom she'd loved or still loved, but none of that made any impression on Alwersik. He had no idea whether her lover was dead now, or her brother, or both of them, or whether they were even real people; in any case they seemed to be far away or part of the past – that's the way it sounded. Besides, she never finished what she started to say. And she said other pretty things, about her girlhood and some bright room or other and about listening to things in secret, which had been one of the things she liked to do.

But up in the camp, there he observed things carefully, nothing escaped him; he'd learned how to interpret things. Like when the conversation was about swimming and diving and Dorian didn't enjoy diving because the rapid fall caused him stomach problems; or on one of the warmer days when they were climbing, along with Stangeler, on the snow-free roof of one of the low earthen barracks for the enlisted men – "I'm so clumsy," said Dorian and tried to climb up the chimney as they had – "You're just imagining it, but don't come up anyway, the thing's starting to wobble," said Alwersik and quickly slid down onto the roof again; Stangeler understood him exactly and did likewise, even though they had been sitting quite comfortably up there on the wide chimney. Or if Dorian said about the heavy, strong, good-humored Ernst von Ress, "He'd certainly like to, just in general, jump right in, but perhaps doesn't think it's right." On any such occasion, Alwersik could figure out exactly when he had to change the emphasis, what needed support, what needed to be defended, and he could also tell how much ground he'd already won there. Of course,

Stangeler looked on in his way, still not entirely without a heavy heart, and took in trivial things that hardly even had a name. Once, when Dorian whacked someone on the head in jest at Café Intim, he came within a hair of having the same expression on his face as Alwersik would have under the same circumstances. Not to mention the language. That was getting to be too much, like his recent statement, "I am coming more and more to the conviction that vagabonds are the only really decent people." He certainly didn't get that from Snobby.

Certain other signs along the way also seemed important to Alwersik. He was sitting in the Turkish casino with Dorian when Snobby came along, sat down with them, and said after a quarter of a minute, "What's all this silence about? Just go right on talking, even if I can't follow all of it, you know I can't most of the time." Beyond that he once even resorted to a clumsy demonstration against Alwersik by addressing Dorian with obvious tenderness and caressing him at the same time. Incidents that indicated a rising tension and simultaneously heightened it occurred more openly every day. Once, over some totally unrelated point or other, Alwersik got an unmistakable look from Snobby; this time when they broke up, things were not smoothed over; neither said goodbye. Alwersik confessed to Stangeler, "Things can't go on this way, sooner or later something's going to happen." At that precise point the student had to give Jan his solemn promise to remain silent, without exception, about everything the latter had said in respect to and about Dorian; Stangeler promised and sensed at the same time that the urgency of Alwersik's demand was a kind of stamp or seal put on what would henceforth be his close association with Dorian. From then on, Alwersik kept things secret from the student as well. Only once did his inner agitation over something that happened force him to open his mouth and he evidently considered it necessary to make an excuse for himself, "I'm really just speaking in general terms, of course," and "you've got to say what's on your mind, and there's no one else I can tell it to." Stangeler backed him up in that regard. Alwersik said, "the guy is so honest and open with me – I really have to pull all my decent traits together, 'garner' all my good qualities. . ."

While all that was going on, it happened that Alwersik, who usually had such a sharp eye and ear for all of Dorian's vital utterances, experienced something that he described to Stangeler – on a different occasion – as the "empty squares" of his own inner life. For instance, if Dorian spoke in a certain way about certain things, for instance about someone's being able to walk without touching the floor, or about living in a room that wasn't in a house, but was sort of suspended in the air, or in a house that wasn't on a street or in any part of the countryside, but just existed all by itself: well, fine, what Alwersik got from all that was that Dorian was in love, loved a girl (well, what else?!), loved her very much, that she was back there at home somewhere (where else whould she be?!) and that he missed her – it was even understandable that he missed her a lot, terribly, painfully. But at the same time, Dorian never said all he had to say, he always broke off, and Alwersik never pressed him to finish, nor did he ever develop a tendency to do so.

In the already milder nights the landscape opened its eyes widely in the moonlight that flooded down, the sky arched deep blue over the widely dispersed roofs of the camp, over town and river, from the steppe over to the forested hills. Now and again the rising wind pushed against the window panes. Along the endless broad corridor, with its row of doors to the right and left, ran Stangeler; then he stopped, his eyes firing into the dense darkness like small caliber artillery pieces; the only bit of light was from a wall lantern all the way at the other end. He, Stangeler, had suddenly realized as he was about to fall asleep, that he was making a basic error: it was as clear as day that only the involuntarily and completely externally gained distance from all his previous, mute life back there, on the other side – in unreality, in his homeland – that only that distance, which he had not really won himself, but which had struck him like the blow of a saber and which he had not inwardly come to terms with – that it was only this that conjured up the possibility of liberation, development, rescue, that even all of that business with writing was only a product of this external chance occurrence and bound up with it, that this life in the camp was something mind-bogglingly extraordinary, and not some generally valid ground like a street in a city or a woods, that perhaps nothing at all could really be done here, nothing brought to its conclusion . . .

Dorian lay there without sleeping, distraught, hot, and listened to the wind that rose, pushed in the casement windows, then released them again. A lament filled him, a vain, pitiful effort to find his way back again; the archway of longing, brittle as glass and just as pure, had previously risen from him and her face,that face, that visage, had flowed back into him from space, like a freely hovering light, entirely part of himself, indivisible, untouchable. But another force, a pressure, that had already troubled him so much, had at first just lightly touched that arch from beneath, then inundated it, then darkened it and then brought it crashing down. And now all that burning longing no longer flowed through that archway, but went off in gloomy, hollowed-out, senseless, undirected waves, without satisfaction, only in sadness. On the next bunk, Snobby was snoring. But Dorian suddenly found a straw to grasp at and perhaps it took only this trivial thing, this being busied with a single, palpable possibility, for him to pull himself together. Efforts had been made more than half a year previously, through the Red Cross or some Danish mission, to re-establish contact with their home country, and he had written his mother, "Take the photograph out of the top left drawer of my desk – it's in a box underneath, the picture of a girl – and send it to me, if you can find a way."

Perhaps it might come. He shuddered, but the feeling was at the same time sweet. Could she, as it were, climb down to the earth? To this earth – foreign earth, with foreign snow, different water, different air, brick buildings. Where did she live? Beyond all this grossness, splendidly isolated, secure – that he felt. But why hadn't he tried to learn more about her then, back then ? He? Then? A different person, boys' clothing; in a sparkling shell, separated from him, stood everything that had passed.

In the same passageway where we saw the Gymnasium student Stangeler worrying about his future,

Aslwersik was simultaneously having his own problems at the other end of the barracks. The passageway ran right through the whole gigantic building, but sometime or other had been partitioned off in the middle with boards in order to stop drafts. Alwersik had been in the theater that evening, without Snobby, without Dorian, and, after the performance, in the company of the actors – in other words, with the theater clique of the camp. There he even met Albert Lehnder, who diverted the conversation when Alwersik mentioned Stangeler. There they were, all sitting in Café Omsk, those men who lived there amidst the pestilential air of the theater (which was also heavily attended by Russians and very profitable), surrounded by jealousy over roles, professional hatred, and intrigues. Alwersik knew this world from other camps. There, too, he'd known the ones who portrayed women – they were always the youngest ensigns and cadets, but his eye may not have been as skilled back then. Here, for the first time, he was suddenly struck by the debased, distorted, hot-house character of those beings, who, after they left the stage and slipped out of their costumes, did not as well descend from the pedestal of assumed gender, but had gradually, in fact, become accustomed to that cloud of subtle tension which the deprivations of all those men about them created. Indeed, there were truly charming creatures among them – the Russian ladies in the theater swore they had to be women, and could only be convinced to the contrary in the dressing rooms, to which they had been led giggling and not at all unwillingly. Thus, in the end, every camp had its acknowledged beauties. For instance, here there was that Angersteiner – no longer a man or boy – can that ever have been a soldier? Nothing but a spoiled, evil person – baser and nastier than any woman has ever been – who fawningly exercised his power.

Alwersik suddenly stuck his arms out in the dark and pounded on his chest with both fists, so that it resounded. Sharply and purposefully his thoughts sprang at the question that suddenly occurred to him. Yes! He was far from being that, he was no robber of souls. Right. But then he glanced off something again, something was still in the dark, like this corridor with the countless doors to the right and left. He paced along it, stopped again, listened: hundreds of sleepers were breathing in and out. He alone was awake; he shuddered. Wake Josip? No. He felt his way along. Now he was in front of the board partition. It was pitch dark here. There were footsteps on the other side. "Hello!" he yelled, but that was senseless – from there on lived only Turks. "Alwersik?" asked Stangeler from the other side. "Were you taking a crap?" said Jan, suddenly happy. "No, not really . . ." They had approached each other closely from either side, both, however, alone so to speak, and in different rooms, separated by the wall of boards. "How're you doing, you old reprobate?" asked Alwersik.

"Well . . ."

"Yob tvoi matj!" cursed Alwersik in Russian, "things are really shitty." As they conversed that way for a little while, they both were free and happy. Then their steps moved away from each other. Their doors squeaked, then it was quiet, except for the snoring and gurgling of the sleepers.

Almost like the blare of trumpets the morning appears at the edge of heaven just a few hours later; to the east the horizon burns in its entire length. The silken span of sky stretches from the steppe over to the forested mountains, the snow on the mountain tops that has thawed during the day and frozen overnight gleams like armor plate.Out on the hills the windows of farm houses are flashing. Like a pink ribbon the frozen river lies there and as the sun heaves itself upward, the snow breaks into myriads of sparkles.

Immediately in the morning, Alwersik felt the events of the evening hanging over him; he was scarcely awake before all that business from yesterday was once again pressing on his chest. He splashed around in the water so that it flew all over and Josip began to curse. Then he went to Café Shubayev for breakfast. He stopped on the steps in front of the gate; it was surprisingly warm, the small square with its little clock tower sparkled in the sun, the air was thin, good-tasting, the most distant mountains lay far back, clear and blue in the absence of wind. A pain took hold of him. He breathed deeply, opened his fur coat, the still, cold air quickly penetrated right to his skin.

It was thawing, dripping.

As he came from breakfast, a man with a goatee ran past, called out to him . . .

"Well?"

"We've just got to get out of here for the summer – men are being hired everywhere – road building – railroad work – cutting wood – but not to the mines, we can skip that – but something, anything – this sitting around in the camp, can't stand it – out there you can eat, live, women! So long." He ran off.

Alwersik took in what he'd heard, was liberated by it, and had even made up his mind already.

The winter dissolved in the shortest time, as it did every year, into a catastrophe of water and mud. The ice in the river broke up – you could hear it. The landscape fell out of white and into brown – no one could have said just when. In four weeks it was warm, in five weeks, dry. The camp swarmed with men. The steppe turned green, summer ran up aginst winter, the tender hesitation of spring was totally lacking here, except perhaps for a few nights that were already long past. Soccer balls went bonking around the parade ground.

But Stangeler did not go bonking along with them. He sat in front of his little wooden table and held parliamentary deliberations; an attempt was being made to bring forth some decision, some direction, from the illuminated and accessible interior whose light was suddenly odd and disconnected, isolated, like the beam of an electric bulb that one has neglected to turn off and is still burning during the day – an attempt was being made to complete this transition in a clear and orderly fashion. It was decided to conclude this and that work (which was difficult, since everything had just been infused with new ideas), it was decided only then to move from a narrow to a broad approach, and consistently. Indeed, this entire governmental plan succeeded even rather well in its execution, it actually succeeded in successfully confronting the whole situation, meeting it head-on. Between the missing laths, through the great, gaping holes in the plank fence, along with the howling wind, the distance broke into the camp from every direction in massive pieces and fragments. And so they turned themselves away from the illuminated interior and toward the landscape once again and over two months arose a situation of excitement, joy, agitation, the probing of possibilities, the forming of groups who wanted to leave together, indeed the whole circle at the Café Intim had figuratively poured out too much and were dripping with plans.

In the midst of all that, Snobby, who hadn't made any plans, simply up and left one day. He had taken a job as an engineer at the boat yard on the river.

Josip Hitschka was playing the role of the powerful agitator: "And I say to you Mr. Secretary . . . ah, pardon me . . . Herr von Valoisky . . . oh, I can never, excuse me please, keep the names straight, naturally I mean Herr Stangeler, no, that's it – Herr von Ress!" he screamed, "I tell you, in principle it doesn't matter *what*. No. Action, life, not theories, morals, textbooks! The whole bunch of you still have textbooks in your heads, that's the problem! We'll live out there! Really work, eat like pigs!"

Alwersik came to Stangeler's room. The scholar was sitting at his little table, surveying the conclusion of his work with satisfaction. "Well, what's up with you, poet? We're out of here in three days! Out to the Sopka. That's one of the mountain forests way over there. We're going to cut wood with the crew led by that Westphalian, Farbade."

"Been registered there for ten days," said the student, "in a work party along with three Turks. The Ress brothers are going too, as a matter of fact, along with several Germans."

Alwersik felt as if he'd had one put over on him – even if relieved at the same time – because he'd just been chatting there, hiding his real intentions, namly simply to disappear with Dorian like Snobby did; and so nothing had been lost by his chatting. The one with the slanting eyes had thought all of this up by himself. He looked past Stangeler.

"Well?"

"Well, I was just thinking, I would like to have torn Dorian completely away from that whole atmosphere, the Café Intim, literature . . ."

Stangeler felt himself totally misunderstood, that false conclusions had been drawn. "Please, I can keep away from both of you as far as that goes."

"Wait, you don't understand me . . ."

"You can . . .," said Stangeler.

Summer had come. One could tell by the three trees in the camp, but also by the woods over there, on the opposite side of the river, which, after a brief period of bright green, had long since darkened. Under the open sky, the work crew had held its last discussion late in the afternoon. Herr Farbade, an estate owner from Westphalia, spoke familiarly and at length about the equipment and tools that they'd obtained, about his plan to really live the rustic life out there, and that he knew all there was to know about wood cutting – at home they cut several thousand cubic meters of timbers for the mines every year. Angersteiner would do the cooking. First Lieutenant Zienhammer, who was the intermediary with the Russians and traveled throughout the country, selling the work of his shamefully underpaid comrades to the Russians and pocketing the profit (in the enlisted men's camp no one was taken in by him anymore) – that man had been there again yesterday evening, everything had been discussed. Farbade recommended that the gentlemen just take all their things along, even easy chairs and tables, trunks – there were enough baggage wagons. Zienhammer had advised the gentlemen quite correctly, he thought – they wouldn't want to come back from the beautiful, green forest anytime soon. "Once you're out there you'll shiver every time you think of the camp!" They'd build huts out there, things would be "splendid" out there! Everyone was excited. Stangeler was not excited; he was inclined to be programmatic.

The horizon glowed, dense and deep red. Out in the fields, Kolchak's soldiers drilled on and on, into the falling dusk. The band hammered out the beat with its drums, the companies of recruits marched in place, trampling the grass flat, singing with completely hoarse throats. They had to sing constantly while drilling and they started shortly after sunrise. Officers were taking their horses over the hurdles.

Two

They are walking beside the carts traveling uphill at a slow pace, some bursting with happiness, others indifferent, some with bedraggled expressions, others worried that something might fall off the creaking vehicles – especially those who took Herr Zienhammer's advice and piled on all their worldly goods. Dorian is walking with Lieutenant Stefani (who has recently taken to wearing a red goatee, of which he is not just a little proud), with the Westphalian, and a one-time German East African who plants his walking stick briskly while strutting along. These gentlemen are in a good mood. They've reached the heights above the city, initially following a curving route over steep roads; now, below and to the right lie the smoking railroad workshops whose overpowering din used to intimidate the passer-by to a certain extent. At the same time, the city is receding from the field of vision farther back to the right. Their somewhat bent-over posture, caused by the intermittent steepness of the road, is relaxed by the green that is flowing down toward them. The eye, intent on the previously sandy ground during the climb, now follows the broad grassy surface in mild surprise. Further on toward the woods, isolated tree trunks are inundated by it, as if in a park. But one is preoccupied with walking – though the pace is more relaxed

– you just keep moving forward, push your knapsack back, breathe, or even . . . talk. In the meantime, the overly broad expanse of the landscape has coalesced all around, no longer broken up by smokestacks or the huts of the suburbs, only by the column with its squeaking carts on the now overgrown wagon path. Towards this company, however, the land rolls in from all sides with its broad contours, overwhelming the senses with its gigantic, scarcely comprehensible mass, which is in part lost on the marchers with their all-too preoccupied, narrow thoughts, surprised as they occasionally may be at it all. But who can resist all of that?! They relax their legs, slow their stride, lift their eyes; out there everything basks in sun-filled distance and passing time and presses upward toward the sky which presses down from above. Only in bits and pieces does it insinuate itself into each breast; but it does indeed penetrate and now it's already demolishing much from back behind and over there, and forcing itself in between, billowing and new, and veiling the episode just finished – that life in the prison camp – quickly, more and more. Like those different appendages on the wagon loads, those teapots and cooking utensils tied on to the bundles, that clank along with the motion of the wagons, the Germans cheerfully accompany every step, every push with conversation: " . . . oughta tie that up on t'other side . . . well look, really . . . nah, I don't know much about that . . . whatta y'call that? . . . crosscut teeth on a saw? . . . all I know about's the teeth in your mouth. . ."

Up front Stangeler lumbered along like a porter, though he had hardly anything to carry; all of his baggage

– a puny rucksack – was piled on a wagon. Alwersik, who'd followed Herr Zienhammer's advice just as little, walked alongside, brisk and erect.

On all sides, the men were urging each other on, cheering each other up.

Dorian is walking beside Stefani, beside the Westphalian and the Afrikaner, but separated from them by the veil woven from the sun, the air, and the rolling, waving blue and green. Here the forest advances with single trees scouting the way, there the meadows flow into it with flat tongues of grass which run off into the billowing green of the underbrush. And in the muted light, oblique sunbeams reach down from the leafy roof. Here the forest has cozy, enclosed spaces like bright rooms, like bright, upper-story rooms with an extensive view over distant, tiny things . . .

The column with its carts has passed by the clearings; the woods are now closing in on the small caravan. The way is becoming steeper.

They rest at noon, and toward evening they call a halt; the column has bored on into the dense green, as far as possible. But no track goes on from here, the forest and its underbrush stand there like a wall. There they unpack. They set up a tent for their tools and supplies. The individual work parties start clearing the underbrush with their axes and building huts with the leafy branches. They carry buckets of water up from the steep ravine. And already dusk is billowing in between the tree trunks like smoke, then sudden darkness, covering even the clearing where, here and there, camp fires are soon flickering. They unhitch the horses – the wagons will not be returning until the following morning. Stangeler is already making coffee with his Turks, the brothers Ress are still working energetically. One of them has made his fire in a long pit; now he has eaten, his fire is out, he stamps out the last embers and spreads the warm ashes in the pit – that's his bed. He pulls his coat over his ears and goes to sleep.

Early next morning when the Westphalian signals the beginning of work with his whistle, they cross the clearing in small squads and disappear in to the forest. Herr Farbade assigns the work-parties and designates the areas where each is to cut the timber. During all of that, there is not a trace of animated discussion on the part of the Germans, thereby awakening a comforting feeling of order and security in the midst of the wilderness. Here and there the tearing crash and dull thump of falling trees can already be heard; they've started and are soon hard at work, with differing abilities and unequal strength. Now everything shrinks down to axes and saws, they stand there two by two, in steaming clouds of their own sweat, their fields of vision narrowed to the movements of their hands. In the meantime the kitchen is being set up in the center of the clearing they've made for camp, a hearth, the kettle, a roof supported on four posts. Dorian is nervous as he works, afraid of not being able to keep up with the others, feels Alwersik's solicitude weighing down on him a little. Whenever the latter asks him, in the course of the first few days, how he's holding up, he says it's child's play – and that's actually the truth, things are going surprisingly easily. Does his comrade doubt that? But now Alwersik even lets him set up the felled trees for sawing alone, something he always tried to take over from him earlier; soon they are no longer doing it together, but alternating – first one, then the other. Stangeler seems to be getting along well with his Turks, judging by his loud guttural croaking.

The landscape reposes in sunny distance and passing time, the forests rest, sunken in on themselves, with their endless rows of birch trunks – a silver keyboard for sunbeams – with their slopes and peaks wandered over by hordes of birches to the edge of heaven, traversed by ravines and brooks, with sudden bursts of floral color in clearings filled with tall swamp grass, with the surprises of the forest, those room-like spaces that suddenly open up then close again as one walks by, with prospects where the landscape falls away quickly and the eye can reach far out to where the forest, on one side, blends into the flat steppes, whose distant stretches seem to stand in whitish haze. And along the thinned-out edge of the forest, the meadows flood in around the individual trees and there are more level paths and, on the rises, farmhouses with windows like eyes gone blind, that nevertheless seem to be staring into the distance, because the greens and blues from afar have been caught in them. Sundays reveal the countryside even more, which otherwise has been limited to ax and saw in heat and sweat. Alwersik always disappears on Sunday – he goes into town. Dorian is free, in a manner of speaking. The Sundays are quiet, beautiful. The Ress brothers, who are in a group with three Germans and Josip Hitschka, have been building a log house in the clearing – it's nearly finished. Sunday afternoons they pound around on the roof, covering it with bark.

The men watch for a while or work a little on their own huts or smoke a pipe with the honorable Germans, with Farbade and the Afrikaner, who says, "Now I've gone and made a mess again with all my crumblets," meaning his pipe tobacco. Up above, in the Westphalian's hut, they keep all sorts of tools, all nice and orderly, everything ready to go, even the sharpening jigs and files. Everyone from the work parties comes to them, mostly because Farbade does a first-class job of restoring a saw, but the big grinding wheel is there as well. It's reassuring. Stangeler makes coffee with his Turks, but the mixture of German, Russian, and French that he speaks with them is hard to listen to. And then there's always something to do on Sundays that you haven't gotten to at the end of a tiring workday – a saw needs to be filed, trousers mended, a hole has to be patched in the roof of a hut, wash water hauled up from the ravine. But with all that, Dorian still finds time to explore the landscape on successive Sundays. On the first walk in the woods, the lushness seems oppressive – so much all at once, after having just three trees in the entire prison camp. A few hundred paces would have sufficed here. But further on, the forest opens out into cleared land and there is the buzzing of bees and a drink of the milk that pours, thick and heavy, from the cold, earthenware jug of the peasant. "Are they giving you enough to eat? What do you get for a cord of wood?" Those are the men's questions. The girls and women merely look on. They have glassy, milky-white skin, full throats and bosoms, and very slim ankles.

Alwersik, who was strolling along the quay on Sunday afternoon with Katia, met up with Stangeler, who was standing around there for some reason or other. This time he was glad to see the slant-eyed one. Because Jan was feeling lazy and satisfied in every respect, but Katia was having one of her more loquacious days and perhaps this could be diverted to inundate the student. So Jan introduced them. They were soon on the course he'd hoped for and Katia was trotting out all the things she loved to talk about, diligently speaking only German, and seemed to be willing to confide in this new acquaintance. Her girlhood in Vienna came up and the business about her brother – finally she'd found someone who didn't know all about it yet, in contradistinction to Alwersik, and so she told the whole story about Camillo – that was his name – about his worrisome, obstinate ways and his precocious intelligence at the tender age of fourteen and about his last days and the letter he wrote to his religion teacher – who taught Catholic catechism at the Gymnasium – just a few days before his suicide. In a loge at the opera, right during the performance of *Rigoletto*, Camillo had shot himself – actually it was during the finale . . . If Katia had observed the student more closely, the flow of her conversation would have stopped dead, because his facial expressions alternated between total distraction and excessive sharpness, sudden sullenness and annoyance. "Good, right, I understood all that," he exclaimed suddenly then, "but I have to ask you, where's the basic difference? Did you ever go for a walk along the Danube Canal in Vienna? Surely . . ." "He was my only brother," Katia rattled on in the same fashion, without being diverted by the student's totally incomprehensible interruptions and questions, "I don't have any other brothers or sisters. It certainly was a strange time, you know, those first weeks after the tragedy, well, maybe it was only just a few days ..." and then, after some sort of nebulous transition, she'd suddenly ended up talking about her husband, who was at the front in the west fighting the Reds and from whom she'd had almost no further news at all. But allowed as how he was really and truly a decent person, her husband. Take the summer of 1918 for instance, in Novo-Nikolaevsk, after the collapse of the Red government in Siberia, when he energetically took the part of the Red Guards who were almost being tortured to death at the time. He actually suceeded in improving the lot of those men, although he was really risking his own position by doing so ... It is impossible to say with certainty whether Stangeler had really listened to her for even a single instant during any of her sad tales; perhaps he was completely preoccupied by the intriguing comparison between the area around the Danube Canal and that near the Yenisei Quay there in Krasnoyarsk, considered "purely theoretically" of course. With an extremely sullen expression he looked out at the mass of water moving by and suddenly took his leave.

Up above the cleared area of the camp, on a hill, there is a space as big as a room surrounded by red firs and the needle-covered ground is as smooth as a polished floor. From there, one can look between the tree trunks far out over the undulating forests to the hazy border of the sky above the steppes. Dorian likes to sit there, does so often. The first few times he had the feeling one does when one arrives in the country – one walks into the bright living room of the country house, green is looking in the windows on all sides, the air tastes fresh, the baggage is standing in the corner. But slowly one really does gain some claim to all that abundance, all that spaciousness, all that freedom that surrounds you, and you walk off here and there. Dorian is walking with a girl on a narrow path that diverges from the edge of the woods; she has nestled her arm against his, she is warm and full, sticks her snub nose into the air, her whole being is like milk. He feels her breast against his arm and is astonished at everything that is happening to him. Now they're standing at a prospect where the forest suddenly falls away more steeply and the eye can gaze far out. In addition to all that, the sun is just sinking. It becomes a sea of fire that glows far back behind them, between the tree trunks. Then he sees the river moving through the landscape way off in the distance, at the border between the mountains and the plains, and discovers that it's the first time he's looked out from here; up till now his excursions have taken him in other directions. The river glows in the sun's last rays.

He does not go into the dusky woods with the girl. On the following Sunday, however, he goes into town with her, which is something she very much wants to do. There they sit in the movie theater and the tea house, then the evening is warm and hazy along the river, the whole quay is swarming with pairs of lovers. It dawns on Dorian that it hasn't taken any real decision to leave behind all those tracks – restrictive and overgrown with thoughts as they all were – leading out of the camp; he can hardly recall them anymore! The water laps at the shore, the river flows by in the evening, the islands appear to be swimming. Right then he sees Alwersik, further on down, disappearing into a street leading from the quay, in female company it would appear, arm in arm.

Well, Dorian is happy that Alwersik hasn't come across him here, with the girl. He's happy, but, of course, gets mad immediately, because what right did Jan have really . . .?

The river drifts away, the couples drift away, the islands swim, the girl is quiet but in good spirits, Dorian is entranced as he watches his blurred recollections drift by. From a great distance, then closer, and then coming quite close, shining forth incomprehensibly from some point or other – the woods and hilltops are dark, the setting sun has shrunk down to a narrow deep-red band – a girl is lying beside Dorian at the edge of the forest and a stranger walks by. Then the massive, white picket fence around a park is shining again in the morning sun, inordinately bright. But now he notices, however, that this is not within him, but is coming from outside – gleaming in front of one of the little wooden houses over there actually is such a bright picket fence.

Night with its sparkling brow was standing watch over the forests when Dorian returned to camp. Around a fire at the upper edge of the clearing sat Stefani, Alwersik, a fat Berliner named Statz, and the elder Ress. He let himself down. They were talking about Berlin, Vienna, about women, about the opera; they gestured, while speaking, with hands that had become coarse and spotted by pitch. They had discovered they had all sorts of things in common. Stefani was just telling about a performance of *Rigoletto* in Vienna, where a Gymnasium student had shot himself in one of the loges – it had just been such a little, popping noise, and hadn't caused much of a stir in the audience; funny, how he'd felt earlier on the same evening that something unusual was awaiting him, he recalled it exactly, he said – that feeling – right while he was shaving. At that time he lived near the opera, in a really nice apartment, as a matter of fact.

Dorian bent over to Alwersik, who was staring past Stefani and into the darkness, and said, excitedly, "Hey, that was the brother of – of the girl, of Katharina, the one I was telling you about, you know – right? I knew him, he was in school with me, we always studied together. His name was Camillo . . ."

They both looked up. In the flickering half-light stood Stangeler, who'd come over unnoticed, had actually been listening to them a good while. He was holding his head hunched down somewhat between his shoulders and watching them both with his obliquely cut eyes. Alwersik made a gesture as if to end the discussion, then interrupted Dorian, stood up, walked away from the fire, and took a few steps toward the dark mass of the edge of the woods. He remained standing there for a long time. . .

The stars twinkle above the inky black of the forest. The last fires turn a dull red, then go out. The camp is asleep.

Three

With the speed of an express train, the storm races across the barren, summery steppe. It remains invisible. There is not a single tree out there, not a bush, to reveal its presence by violent bending and thrashing. Here, however, in the hill country, the full weight of the raging mass of air strikes the forest across a front many kilometers wide. The canopy of foliage foams, the trees lash out with their branches, and soon things begin to crack here and there, then crack again and again as it charges into the woods, roaring, splintering, and crashing. The forest goes mad in the storm.

Alwersik hears the storm coming and sits up. At this point, he is lying with Dorian under the tent that houses the tools. Alwersik is anticipating the violence that he hears off in the distance. He laughs; the nighttime quiet of the camp will soon be all over. Well, let come what may! . . . He slips out quietly, taking care not to awaken Dorian. He steals across the clearing, up to the room among the red firs. There things suddenly become bright blue, every last pine needle on the ground leaps out at the eye, then in the next moment everything is buried in darkness beneath the full weight of the arriving storm and the piercing cracks and deep rumble of the thunder. Nearby, tree trunks are splintering. At the next bolt of lightning, Stangeler pops up at the far side of the clearing. He is grinning. The camp down below has come alive, people are running around, yelling, tying everything down . . .

On the following days the humidity settles over the forests. The moist ground exhales an army of insects, the air seethes with their buzzing. Herds of steers, driven crazy by the stings, their haunches swollen and bloody, come trampling through the woods, their heads to the ground, tails up like flagpoles, and behind them the shepherd, in shirt and trousers, galloping bareback on his horse. His glasses are sitting on the end of his nose – he's a student from Berlin, this shepherd. They all jump out of the way with their saws and axes, the shepherd yells and laughs – and is gone. For the first few days, they try to get some relief by using nets over their faces, but they become sticky with sweat and get in the way, and besides, the mosquitoes sting right through. There are two kinds: the nasty, long-legged ones, with a severe bite that swells and burns and bleeds immediately if scratched, and the others, much more numerous – veils, clouds of them, tiny soft creatures that fill the corners of your eyes, your mouth, your nostrils, your soup; they even get rolled into cigarettes. And the pipe smokers – the Germans, for instance, and Stangeler – stuff them into their pipes, since there's no way to prevent it. Even dense tobacco smoke is no protection from the mosquitoes that hover around the workers in clouds, stick to them. Gloves everywhere, people wrapped up like mummies, faces smeared with pitch and sweat, or scratches and blood. One morning, the Turks come to work stark naked, dark as Moors –

they've smeared themselves all over with pitch. Some say that's dangerous, harmful, yet they seem to tolerate it and get some relief from the insects. Some follow their example.

Alwersik convinces Dorian that rubbing yourself with pitch is nonsense, an unnecessary mess, and that the insects will be gone in a few days. But the plague lasts several weeks.

Alwersik was sitting on the veranda with Katia, looking out over the garden filled with the buzzing of bees. "They were talking about your brother up in camp the other day," he said in an offhanded way, "Yes, Camillo. The one who'd known him was telling about what happened. They'd been talking about the opera, and so the subject just came up by chance – I think it was a schoolmate of his or something like that . . ." He saw how she let her sewing drop a little, bent forward toward him and looked at him, while at the same time her face showed signs of distraction and preoccupation with some thought or other . . .

"What's his name, that one?" she asked quickly. Then there was a pause.

Katia asked the question again.

"Stefani," said Alwersik finally.

She leaned back in her chair again.

They eat like wild men after working. They talk about meat, about good and bad bread, about cabbage and the gas it causes, and a lot about digestion in general. The insects go on buzzing. Magistrate Hampe announces that he's had just about the best crap of his life today while Herr Fleischhanger the school principal is claiming that a certain fern is the best for . . . Stangeler allowed as how these people had finally reached their proper professional level. Constant dissatisfaction reigned despite the plentiful and good food. Their total attention, all the joy of their lives, all their will to live were directed at this one point . . . The steppe stood off in the distance, now constantly enveloped in whitish haze . . . Angersteiner, the cook, who was used to being treated tenderly in the prison camp and on stage, watched with growing apprehension as knightly considerateness disappeared, then found some excuse to go – with the gesture of an enraged prima donna – on strike. The very next morning there was a row and the knightly party proved to be the weaker, and with considerable gusto Angersteiner was sent flying down the ravine and landed with his backside in the water. After him went a trusted friend, after both, a few unambiguous remarks. They came back up boiling with rage, but now no one seemed to want to step out and take them on – the situation had been defused and everyone calmed down. Alwersik, however, who'd been standing there by chance without having been involved earlier, was now attacked by both of them. Four slaps could be heard, as loud as pistol shots, and the cook was reduced to bawling and his knightly defender to cursing. But now things were back under control again and the pair found no further support; in fact, a substitute cook was suggested. An hour later, Angersteiner was standing in front of his soup kettles again.

There were moonlit nights and when the insects were quiet, Alwersik liked to walk through the woods, while Dorian couldn't do without his sleep. Alwersik wandered off, saw the moonlight resting white and satisfied upon the clearing and its beams thrusting through the leafy roof like bars of whitish metal. The great profusion of flowers had been robbed of color and melted down to that same silver. Once he saw Stangeler squatting at the edge of the woods. Alwersik studied him. The face with its slanting eyes had an expression of complete calm as he sat there for the longest time without moving, staring out at the plains. Alwersik suddenly felt himself touched by the presence of the hours together down below in the camp. He would like to have spoken to his comrade.

He would like to have spoken, just to have spoken, he felt a strong need to do so.

But at the same time, Alwersik was disappearing soundlessly into the underbrush.

About this time the last, scattered letters came from home, in roundabout fashion, from Vladivostok to the east. Dorian received a letter from his mother, there in the forest, forwarded from the prison camp; it was nearly half a year old. In the evening after receiving it, Dorian had slipped away to the room among the red firs above the clearing. His heart was beating hard as he broke open the large, stiff, heavy envelope . . . Yes! There were the photographs. The next thing he did was to go loping off to find Alwersik, to show him Katharina's picture. He even took René Stangeler, who was sitting with Alwersik, into his confidence. He wanted to know what Stangeler would have to say about that face, it suddenly seemed very important to know that . . .

He handed the pictures of his mother and sister that had been included to Alwersik first, then the one of Katharina. "That's the one," he said, "how odd that we were just talking about her brother here." Alwersik took the picture somewhat hesitantly, then studied it long and carefully – there was no real movement in his face, other than a very slight sharpening of his bulldog-like expression – then gave it back. He found Katia basically unchanged. Stangeler had turned away. Dorian wanted to hand him the picture. At that point Alwersik touched his arm and shook his head slightly, as if he perhaps wanted to prevent a mistake, a bit of tactlessness on Dorian's part. The latter wanted no part of that, something within him reacted against this sort of tutelage. He said, "Stangeler – what d'you think of this face?" and handed him the picture. Stangeler looked at it, carefully-distractedly, with that somewhat silly expression that his face sometimes had. Alwersik's eyes fastened on him, taking in even the slightest change of expression on the part of the one with the slanted eyes. "A pretty girl . . . a pretty girl," the latter said finally, slowly, then looked up, and encountered Alwersik's look and became confused. "Here in the woods . . . the pretty evening gown . . . in the woods, here in the woods." He got up suddenly, turned away, and ambled across the clearing with his porter's gait and up toward the room among the red firs. Alwersik watched him go. "Completely batty," he mumbled.

They remained quiet for a while, Alwersik and Dorian; then they began to quarrel. "I know myself what to do and what not to do," said Dorian, "I don't need a guardian every time I turn around." "That's not the point, I just don't understand why you had to show it to that slant-eyed slob, it's unreasonable – I don't have anything particularly against him, but . . ." And it went on that way for a while.

On overcast, windless days, the steppe out there seems to be separated off by a gray, iron curtain. On such humid days, the mosquitoes go crazy again, their sound screeches like the singing of a buzzsaw. Dorian is standing with Stangeler near the cooking hut, talking and smoking; but now Alwersik calls from above, from the red-fir room and look, Dorian obeys the call . . . Even the nights are hot now, the moon red . . . One evening an empty mess tin goes flying through the air and into the cooking hut, narrowly missing the cook's head, and splashes into the water barrel. "Idiots!" crows Angersteiner. "That stuff's fit for pigs! You're supposed to eat that? That's supposed to give you strength?" Some work like crazy, but barely accomplish enough piecework to pay for their meals. And so they want a higher piece-rate or higher daily pay. Others work even twice as hard, they start around four in the morning, don't earn very much, but even so, they've already saved something. They are the limiting factor, but now, when they smell the chance of higher profit, they join forces with the dissatisfied ones, because that hurled mess tin immediately set off debates, meetings, a lot of needless talk back and forth.

It was common knowledge by then that, first of all, the front was already located on their side of the Urals (that is, since the capture of Chelyabinsk by the Reds), and second, it had become unstable. It was also known that in the south, starting around Minusinsk, rebellious peasants had opened a second front and were now gradually advancing northward toward Krasnoyarsk in a series of gruesome, small engagements. In the forests far to the south, entire companies of Czech soldiers had supposedly been attacked by the peasants while foraging for food and supplies and strung up on good Russian trees. Alwersik watched René Stangeler, who was crossing the clearing, stared at his broad back, right between the shoulder blades. Hitschka was agitating for a breakout to the south, to link up with the peasants – "live, above all, live, – not just 'experience' – no, no, all that's just literature, but totally crude life, common to everyone, the collective in other words, that's it, that's what matters . . ." Ernst von Ress laughed softly and good-naturedly, more in recognition of Hitschka's eccentricity than from ridicule. Alwersik who was also standing there, said nothing, went on watching Stangeler, and suddenly grinned sourly. "Luckily we've finished building our huts here," said Egon von Ress. And what a sight! Red Austrian cavalry trousers, green puttees, a little pot belly restrained by a gray-green sweater, pince nez, and full beard. The Germans considered everything objectively and calmly, as if they were sitting over beer and cigarettes; even they raised the question of going on strike. That was discussed heatedly. At the mere mention of the subject, people started yelling, insulting each other's honor, but the modest attempt of several conservative men to restrain things in an old-fashioned way called forth peals of laughter, but also certain challenges on the part of both parties, challenges which the merchant Statz from Berlin termed "South German presumptuousness."

Alwersik had just come from Katia. He had gone to the movies with her, had – almost for spite – gone out with her again anyway, and had seen ghosts: fifteen Stangelers, twelve Dorians, each one of whom had seemed real for several minutes of torment, until, each time, the illusion vanished. He walked down the Bolshaya, out to the marketplace, through the park. On a park bench on a quiet side path, Dorian was sitting with a girl, showing no signs of tenderness of course, and they were well separated from each other, but in animated conversation. Deep relief, but even deeper annoyance for Alwersik. Take a deep breath – but even so, a groan under yet another burden. He slipped back unseen. But he did not hike back to the Sopka. He stayed in the city for the night. It was unthinkable to lose Katia. And it was equally unthinkable to lose Dorian. Caught between these two impossibilities, he hurled his schnaps glass against the dirty table top.

First a gigantic, gaunt, old nag appeared at the bend in the road, then the tiny, two-wheeled wagon could be seen, on which squatted the tall, skinny Lieutenant Zienhammer. He was coming to pay a visit to the malcontents. The latter were all sitting together and had just finished wolfing down their food. He faced a resolute group. Speakers came forth, among them Fleischhanger the school principal. It became evident, however, that these speakers would have been put to better use cutting wood. Angersteiner stood off to the side, graceful and refined. Alwersik had not yet returned from town. The speakers all had the same thing to say, interrupted each other constantly, and ended up quarreling among themselves. Zienhammer then spoke at length, rapidly, monotonously, deadeningly. In the end they were, almost without exception, convinced that especially favorable working conditions and wages prevailed up there on the Sopka, which could only be attributed to the special benevolence of Zienhammer, who was obviously expending his entire affection on that particular working party. Oh! You should just see how things are elsewhere! Suddenly voices were heard that described the piece-work rate as right and proper, that proudly announced that they'd already saved a hundred, a hundred and fifty rubles, you just had to work! Men turned up then who even went so far as to accompany the lieutenant part way back to town, chatting amiably, with two of them leading the wagon behind. It was all quite chummy. That in the forseeable future it would unfortunately be scarcely possible for them to get wagons up there to transport their belongings – Zienhammer had said "effects" – that the lieutenant had mentioned while leaving. He would, of course, do everything he could for the gentlemen who did not want to stay there under any circumstances – but they should really all stay there, what was there for them down below? Nothing good, bad times were coming, life up there was a hundred times healthier than in the prison camp. And this was happily endorsed by all.

The moon came up early, ponderous and reddish. The hills and valleys turned toward it, glowing in splendor. Stangeler and Dorian stood in the moonlight, then walked a few paces farther. The path was segmented by the shadows cast by the trees. "That's just it," said Dorian, "I had the feeling with all this that I . . . finally recognized . . . despite the enormous separation from everything back in the past . . . this unity of all life, there and here . . . and that there is basically no such thing as . . . adventurous and extraordinary . . . and that nothing happens by chance . . ."

"You didn't," said Stangeler rather obstinately, "completely understand all that, when I . . . possibly I didn't make my self clear enough . . ."

With a rustling noise, Alwersik jumped out of the bushes and onto the path. He had been right next to the other two. "Philosophy! Philosophers!" he yelled. Dorian looked to the side with a distressed expression. Jan tried to penetrate the weave of moonlight, tried to make out the features of the two exactly. . .

Suddenly he was struck rather hard by the perfectly obvious fact that it would be totally impossible to constantly interrupt this Stangeler – at just the right time and as if by chance – every time there was such a meeting and incipient discussion between these two . . .

Besides, perhaps Stangeler even felt a "duty" . . .? no, certainly not that. Certainly slanty-eyes was not that strait-laced . . . Nevertheless! Perhaps he thought it was necessary . . . right . . . Could that be the right way to look at it?!

The peasants sent gloomy looks their way, the mushroom pickers avoided the camp, passing it off to the side. A sort of emptiness arose – and into it soon murmured rumors, a spring that never ran dry, that now suddenly began to well over. Only when Hussein – an Albanian Turk, a captain who worked in the same group with Stangeler – returned from the prison camp was light shed on the situation. Hussein had disappeared for three days and now turned up again.

Six hundred young Russian recruits had mutinied up at the barracks near Gorodok, had attacked the city and engaged the Czechs, banking prematurely on the arrival of the peasants from the south.

Those six hundred men, who'd been overwhelmed and then surrendered in hopes of clemency, were all executed, six hundred men, slaughtered out in the meadows like animals.

From the first sign of dawn until night fell, that's how long the salvos of rifle fire lasted.

Hussein's eyeballs stood out white against his brown face. He'd seen everything. They'd shot nine Hungarian officers from the camp on suspicion of having been the instigators. Perhaps it would come to an actual decimation in the camp – every tenth man would end up in front of the rifles.

The war prisoners were at the bottom of everything – that's what the Czechs were telling the populace.

Any prisoner found outside the barbed wire in the vicinity of the camp would be shot on sight.

And he, Hussein? "Oh, terribly . . . but well hidden . . . Cossacks everywhere." Hussein went on to describe in detail, with violent gestures, the execution of the nine officers. The Czechs had led the condemned men out of the camp to the north, ordered them to walk toward the steppe in a row and shot them down from behind after perhaps a hundred paces. This was, in fact, the usual way of carrying out the death penalty in the Russian Civil War.

That evening, when the fires were already burning – though more modestly than usual – there was rustling and cracking noise at one spot in the woods. Six riders broke out into the clearing and rode up to the cooking hut. There they stopped, motionless on their horses, illuminated by the glow of the fires. Their rifles lay ready across their arms.

Everyone just squatted there quietly. The patrol suddenly turned away, rode onto the sunken road, and down toward the city.

Even that passed, though it made itself felt for a long time afterward. Nevertheless, ten days later, the officials from the city were out there again, walking over the clear-cut hilltops, measuring the wood piles, handing out the wages. They even reassured the workers. This was especially necessary for some, for instance the woodcutters Fleischhanger and Hampe. The faces of the Russians were quite gloomy. But it passed. The mosquitoes stayed, and the summertime haze hung over the steppe beyond, untouched by a single breath of air. Hitschka went back to talking, with clenched fists. Stangeler grinned at him.

"What's up with you?" asked Alwersik. "You in love? Watch yourself, a lot of the women around here have venereal diseases."

"Aw, c'mon, no . . ."

"Well, I just saw you in the park a bit ago, and somewhere else, too . . ."

"Worry about you own love affairs, Jan, everyone has to figure out for himself what he's going to risk in that regard . . . but I have worse things to worry about than dumb stuff like that, thank God."

"Don't let that Stangeler fill your head with funny ideas."

"How so – what's with you and Stangeler all the time . . .?"

"Just tell me, Dorian, what's bothering you. You're going around . . ."

"OK. Certain experiences recently have shown me that we're . . . in a manner of speaking . . . not at all so incredibly far removed from all of our previous lives, back home, I mean . . . well, how can I describe it to you . . ." Alwersik's eyes suddenly went blank, as with fright. "Yeh, and then . . ." Dorian went on talking, "I've never missed a single person as much as I do now. It comes from all of this nature around here . . . I think . . . this terrible longing, it's something new . . . I already mentioned it to you a lot in camp, but you were probably too busy . . ."

Alwersik had gotten up slowly from the grass, his chest cage expanded, his eyes glowed . . . freedom from everything . . . simple, just the way that tree there is standing in front of your nose, and another one there, and between them the sunbeams on the ground . . . nothing to keep you from walking right between them . . . get rid of the evil, clean things up, put everything in order! And just go on happily rowing your boat through life. What're you doing hanging around here?!! . . . But now he sits down again; really, you might say he collapsed in a heap onto his previous place.

"Maybe that's because you have her picture now," he said after a while without much force to his words. Then they fell silent. For several moments during their conversation, they'd forgotten to wave the mosquitoes away; now the bites burned and swelled.

Now and again one of them took a few days off; then the remaining partner of the sawing team paired up with someone else whose partner was also taking time off. Alwersik worked hard to convince Dorian to get some to rest. Stangeler had just lost his partner a few days previously. He was a Hungarian who, now that he had all this freedom, had gone crazy over women after such a long period of deprivation. Hurrying from peasant girl to peasant girl, he'd finally completely disappeared from the woodcutting camp and found a job as a hired hand out in the hill country. And so it happened that Alwersik walked into the forest with the slant-eyed one on the following morning. They worked in silence without taking a break and by evening had leveled an extraordinary number of trees.

The heat and the mosquitoes had reached the boiling point. Small fires had been started, heaped with wet wood and leaves, so that everyone was working in a thick cloud of smoke – otherwise they'd have gone crazy. But even so, there were plenty of bites, and Stangeler spit out, in a rage, a mixture of bugs and tobacco juice. Dusk came swimming in between the tree trunks. They were trying to get a head start on the next day's work, swiftly felling one more row of trees so that they could cut them up first thing in the morning. Now they were hurriedly chopping off all the limbs. Alwersik's bulldog face was drawn together like a clenched fist as he jumped along the trunks, hacking off branches. He was filled with the irritating torment of someone who has been waiting in vain for something, for a day, then another day, then yet another and now comes yet another evening, empty and calm, there's nothing there, just the crude outline of the slant-eyed one, showing him his behind every time he bends over to trim off a branch, then straightens up again and takes a step backward . . .

Alwersik swung his axe at the next branch, with a careless, lackadaisical motion that expressed his burgeoning desperation. As he struck, something dark and shadowy moved near him in the dim light, the sharp blade bit easily and with a thud into Stangeler's back as he stood up. The slant-eyed one pitched forward clumsily into the brush, half turned to the right, breaking the branches or pushing them aside with his broad shoulders.

Alwersik ran, shouting. Their comrades arrived, lifted up the groaning boy. Alwersik ran in the direction of the camp. In the red-fir room, he stopped for the duration of the blink of an eye. In the falling dusk everything was bluish, distant. His heart was pounding like a hammer, the blood roaring in his ears, he was still holding the ax clenched in his hand – even in his fright, he hadn't let it fall. His jaws bit against each other like screw clamps. But then his gaze chanced upon the edge of the sky far out beyond . . . and he saw fire.

The horizon was aflame. At first licking forward almost imperceptibly, then blazing up in broad strips, a prairie fire was on the move. What usually was hidden from the eye by the haze out there, veiled until it sank back into evening, now seemed to blaze up in clarity – the distance. And even if that fire had its origin in the most peaceful of purposes – set by the farmers when the wind turned toward the steppe as a precaution against the spontaneous igniting of the dry grass – nevertheless, the glow on the horizon summoned up a further realization on Jan's part: the country was in the middle of a war, a wild, cruel war – *that's* what it meant.

There were several thunderstorms in the following days. The forest sighed and dripped in the rain. Afterward, it turned noticeably cooler. Mosquitoes no longer sang in one's ear; they had all disappeared, were gobbled up, gone. With the insects no longer buzzing, it seemed extraordinarily quiet. The birch trees formed a silver keyboard for the sunbeams as they marched off into the distance, letting through ample light and pale sky. The cut-over slopes exhaled the smell of pitch into the open prospects. Out beyond lay the steppe, completely free of haze; from the red-fir room, you could see clearly to its farthest border.

Yes, things had become quieter on the Sopka. At the same time that Stangeler had been taken to the infirmary after the accident, others had departed as well, that is, those who had not taken Herr Zienhammer's advice, but instead had hoisted their light packs onto their shoulders. The work had gradually progressed, uphill and down, far beyond the summits and now the forests stood out against the sky, deeply split and leveled stepwise. Everywhere resinous piles of wood trailed off along the edges of the hills in long columns and already the clang of the axes had to echo from a considerable distance across those clearings and back to camp.

Between Alwersik and Dorian silence reigned, although Jan, especially toward others, now actually tended toward loquaciousness. He had, for the first time, taken a few days off from work and now Dorian was sawing with a reddish-blond German.

Alwersik slipped into the tent with the tools. It was empty and quiet there, everyone was at work. He shouldered his light rucksack, which was already packed, and left. He marched into town, obtained the desired discharge papers at the city hall, but did not return, as prescribed, to the prison camp, but instead walked down to the harbor. Here a steamer was loading wood, but the work was taking too long – there were only three men. Alwersik pitched in, helped, impressed them with his strength, won them over with his laugh and his bad Russian. He left on the steamer that evening, as a loader and stoker. The ship headed upstream, in the direction of Minusinsk.

Angersteiner spread the news when they asked about Alwersik. The latter had yelled to him as he passed the cooking hut that he was off, not to the camp, but in search of other work. Dorian had to keep it all to himself, couldn't talk about it with anyone else. He would have preferred to speak to the younger Ress. Actually, he felt relieved, like he'd been reborn.

Alwersik was lying on his back, on the foredeck of the ship, looking straight overhead into the night sky. The stars sparkled. The ship bore on. The forests on either shore accompanied it. He felt at home in that situation, the way he was lying there on the moving ship, looking at the sky, not knowing what was coming next – life was so easy to grab hold of! – whether here or somewhere else, near or far – you just had to go on merrily rowing your boat. He was delighted.

At the same time he had the dim recollection that, on his way to the harbor where he'd later found this ship, he'd walked close by Katia's house – and that his proximity to it hadn't dawned on him at the time. He tried to reflect on this at least a little, but it didn't work; he simply couldn't get hold of it. He didn't think about Dorian.

Then, as the ship bore on, he thought about the Sopka in general and about a certain diminution and disappearance of tension – he now actually relaxed his right arm and finally opened his hand, which had been slightly clenched into a fist.

In the streets of Krasnoyarsk now, a few townspeople could often be seen standing together here and there, talking with heads lowered. If an officer came by, they'd fall silent. In the evenings the workers from the railroad workshops would not disperse immediately after passing through the great, gray gates; their troops seemed to resist splitting up, did so only gradually, then walked on in sixes and sevens. Newspapers were hardly looked at, indeed were almost pushed away with hostility. The important news was now being obtained from other springs, babbling ones that never dried up. Actually they were now growing into rivers, torrents.

Fall was waiting, far out on the steppe, and in the forests and mountains on the far side of the river. The tiny windows of the farmhouses in the hill country blinked sleepily, kilometers away. Katia felt as if she would dissolve and fall apart in every direction or had to run away from the city in fright at the end of every street, run away from the emptiness of her own heart; and yet at the same time she felt feverish and was animated and open right down the the last fiber of her body wall, which enclosed nothing but agitation.

News of her husband? – nothing.

Jan – what had happened there?

And at the same time, you heard about some terrible thing and had barely managed to pass it off as rumor when it came, hardened into truth, clanking into the house by the back door.

Once, when she was sitting in the little garden where the bees were still humming, her pain broke through its fetters and she groaned and sobbed and gulped for two hours without stopping, like a cow that was choking. And suddenly fear came to her. She ran into her room, thrashed around in bed, screaming. Something frightful was coming, she knew it as realistically as if it had already happened – much more terrible than anything a human could possibly bear, steam rollers, landslides of horror, terror, such that one could only howl and scream, oh, she was being thrown into fire, everything was burning all around her. Right now, in the midst of that colossal steppe landscape, it was just as if one were sitting helplessly on a huge, bone-dry chunk of peat that was being ignited from all sides. Fire! The horizon is burning! She started up wildly, angrily now, animal, defiant, talons . . .

But nothing, silence. A bird whistled, a bee hummed on its way past the garden door, silence, a bit of wind, a tiny bit of frail sun's warmth blowing by, that was all.

She stared straight ahead. Some sort of image sank diagonally across her mind's eye, another one, then nothing, emptiness, red spots on the inner surface of her eyelids. And then suddenly it was standing there in her mind, a genuine, antique Russian tea service, vivid crimson, with a sugar bowl in a wild, barbarian shape, with a brick-red zigzag pattern . . . like an exotic, gruesome house somewhere in the east, a house or temple where people are killed, sacrificed . . .

Then she sobbed and whimpered softly to herself. It was the uncertain, the most deep-seated and evil horror. It was a very bad time.

Alwersik was standing in the woods. The night was

congealing among the tree trunks. For just the shortest time, he could still see the dim lights of the steamer on the river now and again. After the wood had been unloaded, shortly before departure, he had left the ship unnoticed by a gangplank that was still in place. His small rucksack lay at his feet. He took out the wool blanket, crept into the bushes, bedded down, ate his fill, had a satisfying smoke, and then went to sleep. After just three hours' march, morning saw the forest open out upon a broad hollow with low hills and farmland. The village beckoned amicably to Alwersik from down below. An hour later he was a hired hand, had a roof over his head, a bed, and a bowl to eat from. Everything was cheerful and matter-of-fact; the harvest was already in, and so the work was light there, child's play for him after cutting wood. There was a humorous side, too. The old peasant woman squatted down on the very top of the manure pile, pulled up her skirts and passed her water. Alwersik, standing down below, did the same. When he happened by chance to glance upward, hardly likely in order to feast his gaze upon the charms being displayed, she called down to him in her sonorous language, giving a friendly wag of her finger, "Oh, you bad boy!" He doubled up with laughter. Anyway, Alwersik did have his share of women there, too, all the more since there were strikingly few young men. Just to carry things to the extreme, he gave lessons to the starost's daughter and several other lumbering ladies in . . . French. Those hours were exquisite – he had the feeling that he was in the act of taking several cows for a walk across the Place d'Etoile in Paris. Be that as it may, the girls were smart and learned quickly. He stayed there for several weeks, learned to speak Russian better, and kept his eyes and ears open.

From what he learned, though the village had indeed sided with the rebellious peasants, it lay beyond the planned line of attack. Because they had no intention of proceeding toward Krasnoyarsk along the river, but well to the side of that artery so as to have the cover of the dense, ravine-filled forest as long as possible. The virgin forest extended towards the north in a different direction than right along the Yenisei. For that reason, Alwersik left the village. He was carrying a heavy load of provisions. On the third night, he was sleeping extremely deeply. Stangeler was holding out toward him – his eyes slanting even more from his sarcastic grin – Katia's photograph. He struck out at the image with his fist, whose bones had changed into a sharp blade and cut it down the middle. But nothing happened. It had to be burned, the way one set fire to the driy grass with a burning piece of cardboard, so that everything would disappear once and for all behind the flaming horizon. But Stangeler had an arm made for grabbing things, as long as a gorilla's; the huge, cruel hand at the end of it came closer and closer to his throat and now began to exert a pressure that became more and more unbearable. He yelled and reared up but was immediately pushed back down.

The transition to wakefulness and the light of day was brief, and now, standing there, were . . . Cossacks. In other words, the end.

But then: red stars on their caps. What was going on?

He was bellowed at while six pistols were pointed in his direction: "Where to? Where from? What are you going to do there?"

Thank God for the weeks in the village. Thank God he could speak Russian!

He stood up, hands held high. They searched him, went through his rucksack. Then he simply told them the truth, underscoring this and that – the murder of his comrades and the six hundred recruits, the hard work up on the Sopka for such wretched pay. He also said that up there they'd already thought about – and here he'd recalled Hitschka's speech – breaking out and making their way to the south to join up with the advancing peasants. Finally he told them he wanted to fight, against the Whites, but especially against the Czechs – just came out with it suddenly, actually without any very clear intention – yes, row, row, row your boat!

Could he ride?

He said that he'd served with an Austrian cavalry regiment. He could see clearly that his statement earned him considerable respect. They walked away from him, considered the matter. Then, without wasting words, they told him what was going on. Yesterday they'd finished off a small Czech cavalry patrol. There were the horses they'd taken. They were making it difficult to get anywhere. Would he consider following them with three of the horses on a line? At the slightest suspicious movement, they'd cut him down immediately.

"Certainly." They walked two hundred paces into the woods, then the horses could be heard. There they stood, a rider nearby with his rifle over his arm. They mounted up; Alwersik had to ride in the middle, with the three horses roped together. They rode almost the entire day.

All the while, Jan was subjected to a sort of cross examination. Toward evening, in a broad clearing, the commander pointed to the edge of the woods on the opposite side and said to Alwersik with a grin, " Take . . . whatever you need!" At the same time, they all took their rifles from their shoulders and now, as he rode somewhat hesitantly across the clearing and glanced back, he saw the six barrels aimed at him. Then he shivered suddenly, once again the end caressed him, because he was thinking of his dead comrades, those nine officers from the camp at Krasnoyarsk who'd been told to walk out into the steppe. Then someone called to him from behind and pointed with his arm, "Farther to the right, farther to the right!"

So *that* was it! There lay the dead Czech cavalrymen. Their boots were almost new, their riding pants in good condition.

After he had equipped himself with boots, trousers, and various belts, he was allowed to pick out a horse and was given weapons. Then they made him swear an oath and he spoke words like "Death to Kolchak!" and " Death to the Czech bloodsuckers!"

And with that, he was taken into one of those isolated Cossack bands that were not fighting on the side of the reaction but, cut off here, were making common cause with the south Siberian peasants.

Alwersik proved his mettle within a few weeks of his being recruited into the troop.

Katia had to feel for firm ground, since everything was unstable, slipping away, and she found a toehold by going to the hospital as a nurses' aide. And she was lucky, because she was sent – just as a helper, to be sure – to a surgical ward, where they needed hands just then, since streams of wounded were being sent back from the front once again. Her husband was not among them, nor anyone who knew him. That she was there and remained there was the important point, because later on, with winter, came typhus and the newly recruited assisants were all sent to the contagious disease hospitals. Since Katia had never learned how to be a physician's assistant, she was at first assigned to the admissions office and later as a nurse in a convalescent ward.

Toward the end of the month of September she finally had a weekday off. She had become a stranger to her home, rarely spending any time there now, sleeping in the hospital for the most part. Now she awakened in the morning within her own four walls. It was still warm and summery, the garden quiet, however; the humming of the bees was missing, everything seemed to collapsed upon itself like a veil - and indeed the luxuriousness of summer was shriveling, retreating everywhere. No longer did mists hover, the vistas were cold, the foreground appeared sharper. After she had had her tea, she went on her way, to the Sopka, of course. It was a beautiful day, but she scarcely noticed that, because it was a day full of anxiety that enclosed her almost entirely. But from all sides the land undulates toward the walker in broad waves, showering the senses with gigantic, scarcely comprehensible masses, which, no doubt, simply glance off in part. But who can totally resist all that? Her limbs relax, her pace slows, her eyes are lifted upwards. Out there everything basks in the sun-filled distance and passing time, and arches upward toward the sky which presses down from above. Only in bits and pieces does it insinuate its way into her breast, but it does indeed penetrate, it does indeed loosen for a while the ring of sadness that has closed around it. Here, now, is the forest already, with individual trees scouting the way; there the meadows flow into it, tongues of grass in the shadows. Here the forest has cozy, enclosed spaces like rooms, like bright, upper-story rooms, with an extensive view. She leaves the path, walks into such a bright forest room, and has a closed-off feeling, as if the bushes were coming together and filling in behind her, as if she had entered the clearing through a door and this door had now closed itself behind her. Now she would not be too afraid of footsteps in the woods – such a noise would seem to her to be coming from the room next door, from which one is completely separated by the wall.

Up above, Angersteiner told her that Alwersik had long since left camp, had gone to look for other work, no idea where. She stood there beside the cooking hut, that fellow in his rolled-up shirtsleeves in front of her. With a sad gaze, she studied the beautiful log cabin that the Ress brothers and the Germans had built. Then she looked out toward the slopes with the piles of timber trailing off across them. From far off, the blows of axes echoed across to the camp. She supported herself against one of the uprights of the cooking hut with her hand, then turned, said goodbye, and walked off, occupied only by the relaxed pace of her legs, suffused by the mild warmth of the sun.

But she still made inquiries at the prison camp that very same day: no, he wasn't there either.

A few days after Katia's visit to the Sopka, Dorian moved back down from there and into the camp again.

Four

The horizon was aflame. Like a prairie fire migrating before the wind in broad, fiery strips, ignited here and there, far ahead, when the wind sends burning bundles of grass flying into areas not yet reached, thus causing countless, individual outbreaks everywhere, far in front of the reddish glow of the main conflagration – in that way the advance of the Fifth Soviet Army followed its course toward the east with ever-increasing speed, before which the forces of Kolchak, the Czechs, and the Entente melted away, while those of their pursuing enemy grew inexorably. Because everywhere throughout the land, long before the arrival of the red wave, the long-suffering peasants rose up, formed so-called "partisan bands," and fell upon their foreign oppressors. In some cities, as soon as the retreating front approached, the workers seized power and refused to admit the Whites who were falling back; in fact, in many locations, after they had overthrown or killed their commanders, the garrisons marched out under the red banner to link up with the victorious Fifth Army. Racing ahead of the local revolutions were the rising floodwaters of rumor. Just a babbling spring at first, then a swelling torrent which then finally, at the moment of open rebellion, plunges into the millraces of passion to provide the driving force. The horizon was burning. Like a flaming mountain range of wreckage and human bodies, the front and the chaos that welled up before it migrated across the immeasurable breadth of the land, from west to east.

Indeed, as if to increase the already victorious enemy's lust for battle to the extreme, men became devils in the desperation of the generalized collapse; and during the last hours that they still held power and in the very face of certain revenge, acts of insane cruelty were still being carried out and the blood of those suspected of sympathizing with the Red adversary flowed in streams. The South Slavic Legion - mainly Serbs, not really large in number but occasionally exceeding even the Czechs in bestiality - had gotten the notion of executing captured Bolsheviks gradually, in a manner of speaking, by, after the men had been taken to the site where they were to be dispatched - it was at the edge of the city of Semipalatinsk in Western Siberia - hacking off a limb at random, then coming back after two hours and repeating the procedure, thus prolonging their enjoyment by killing incrementally. This happened not far from homes that were being lived in and the horror of the unbearable screams of the victims caused the inhabitants of the closest part of town to flee as soon as such a column approached the place of execution. But, after the capture of Semipalatinsk, a large number of those Serbs were caught by the Red troops and the tormenters came to the end that they themselves had invented. With his mass shootings of recruits, Gajda, the leader of the Czech Legion, had made himself notorious, particularly in the summer of 1919. But from the very beginning he hardly stood alone in that regard. Shortly before the Fourth Soviet Army took Samara on the eighth of October, 1918, the Russian General Lupov had 900 Russian recruits shot when they refused to march out along with the Whites who were evacuating the city. A little later, at Ufa on the twenty second of October, Lupov regaled a group of military leaders at length with his accomplishment.

By the fall of 1918 the Czech attack in the Volga region had already been brought to a standstill by the successful operations of the First, Fourth, and Fifth Soviet Armies and the Red front had clearly been solidified by the occupation of Kazan, Simbirsk, and Samara. Removal of the closest and most serious danger to Moscow had been the purpose of the campaign on the Volga and this task had now been fulfilled. After the capture of Samara, the advance came to a halt and, while a somewhat nebulous constitutional convention met at Ufa to create a legal framework for the new "White Russia," Kolchak, who could hardly have cared less about all that, was able to prepare his dictatorship, which he then proclaimed in Omsk on the eighteenth of November, supported in the main by the Czechs and the English. Simultaneously, however, he used this time of relative quiet at the front to build up his army. The reasons that the Red troops did not immediately continue their advance beyond Samara were, first, that significant numbers of men had to be shifted to the southern front – and from then on, against General Denikin – and secondly, the Red troops were increasingly faced by serious opposition from the newly formed "Officers Divisions" of the White Army. These were elite battle units, consisting exclusively of officers who were serving as ordinary riflemen because of their beliefs. They made things incredibly difficult for the Reds beyond the northern Urals, and their self-sacrifice and extraordinary daring in battle made possible, at first, the continued occupation of the industrial centers there, above all, Perm, which, nevertheless, in the course of events after the breakthrough of the Soviet troops at Ufa in June of 1919, " . . . was relinquished to the Reds without a fight," as General Sacharov, then the Chief of Staff of the White Army, emphasized - without mentioning bitterly at the same time the factories, the huge stores of provisions and other military supplies and the entire Kama River flotilla. With that, one can see how men and materials steadily accrued to the Soviet armies during their advance toward the east.

That advance did not actually begin until the spring of 1919. It was much less the winter - which in the Russian Civil War hardly ever brought about a real lull in the fighting - than the already mentioned two circumstances that had delayed the campaign until than. Scarcely a year had slipped away since that second of June 1918, when Leo Trotsky - to the resolute horror of all party comrades - had dared to call to arms all of the former Imperial Russian professional officers within the Soviet zone, since those days when the first Soviet army (Tukhashevski) was formed at Simbirsk, since those days when Trotsky had started to organize, build up, and above all, bring discipline to a previously nonexistent Red fighting force - and that, one could almost say, in the face of enemy fire. Every bit of counterrevolutionary treason at the front – and such things did happen, of course – was laid at Trotsky's feet since then, precisely because of that measure; and yet, it was the only possible way to make soldiers, to form an army from Red Guards and various bands and troops. Those officers contributed hugely to the Red cause, and among them were not a few who clearly recognized on which side one had to fight with determination as a Russian and that the freedom and independence of their fatherland was not truly being defended by those who permitted their so splendid and modest people to be humiliated in front of the English and French and to be mistreated by the Czechs. But how curiously the nation had split itself! Peasants fought on this side and on the other side as well – even if, under Kolchak, more from forced conscription than loyalty to the White flag. Officers and "intelligentsia" fought on this side and over there – even if, under Trotsky, for the most part from the pressure of the call-up rather than the Red flag. But by and large the peasant population showed that they, rather than the "educated folk," properly, even if dimly, comprehended the historical future of their great nation. Constant mutinies, desertion to the Reds in closed formations, hundredfold martyrdom of Kolchak's disobedient recruits, a martyrdom without actual conscious decision – such things accompanied the rise and fall of the reaction, showing more and more clearly the new course that the gigantic body of the people was setting, as ponderously as a huge ship coming about, but nonetheless with increasing certainly. Indeed, physiognomy often decided. Truthfully, things were just that simple in many a decisive moment. That is to say, some Grigor Petrovich, who, with his surpassingly stupid expression, was listening intently to some orator or other, while his low but honest brow, his tousled blond hair, the depths of his blue eyes, his strong body more than clearly bespoke the entire future, more than clearly said whose unknown soldier he was – to such a Grigor, Nicolai, or Vassily, some Bolshevik peasant agitator who tossed back his bearded apostle's head and poured out wild speeches against the state, church, religion, capital, and landowners – to such a Grigor, Ilya, or Piotr it was exactly this orator, whose words he scarcely understood at all, who seemed closer, better, more familiar, and warmer than the well-shaven, dead impenetrability of an English or American face (to say nothing of the Japanese), even if they were urgently emphasizing that they were the ones who were defending his real fatherland, his real religion, his mother earth and the peasants against the Red antichrist. And this basic physiognomic inclination was likely to be all the more confirmed and abetted when some English detachment came marching haughtily into a village to search for weapons – on this, as indeed on all occasions, confronting the Russian peasant with the very same condescension they displayed in their colored colonies – or even more, when the Czechs plundered and, in doing so, shot down a dozen men in the twinkling of an eye.

In the spring of 1919 Trotsky drew for the decisive blow the sword which he had been sharpening for an entire year. In well-ordered ranks the Fifth Army stood before the Volga, blond soldiers, poor as Franciscans. By means of millionfold words, posters, and writings, the communist ideology attempted to bore its way into peasant skulls. Indeed it was, it seemed, actually willingly taken up. But that was precisely their leaders' mistake – certainly not one of the little ones that we little people make, but a mighty, a heroic mistake. Thus erred a Trotsky. Because, for all the sharpness of his intellect, his eyes remained fixed – as is quite proper for all men of action – his eyes remained fixed, so that he would not be paralyzed, on what was actually taking place. Basically invisible to him and his "comrades" was the gigantic, dark, shadowy something which mutely shoved its way in behind all the rational and understandable, accepted and convincing, theoretical and practical, beneficent and futuristic machinations of the party. Because there was a new figure on stage, an almost eternal figure – eternal, that is, in comparison to the limited life span of an economic conviction, even if the latter claimed to encompass the world! It stood behind all that henceforth, lending its mass and momentum, lending its strength for a time, as a guest, as the guest of the flag that had to serve there just for a limited time – and this Red flag only now became something to be feared when the peasant took the temporal and transitory into his – by comparison – almost eternal hands. Thus Trotsky served – deceived by his exalted destiny in an exalted way – thus he, the non-Russian, the international, the intellectual, the ideologue, served in the end, despite all the programmatic noise in the foreground, the slow, dim destiny, that only now, in the midst of all that busyness began to sleepily raise its heavy eyelids, then awakened in those millions unversed in reading and writing; awakened – and the first words that it bore, felt more than explicitly thought, in the midst of all the blather of the freethinkers, may well have been, "Out with all those godless foreigners, out of Russia, once and for all with those enemies of Christ!" Thus was Russia's new age ushered in. But this introduction was not permitted to be recognized at the time as simply an introduction. It was only recognized as such when the so-called world revolution failed to occur. And it seems to have been symbolically terminated by the expulsion of Leo Trotsky from the territories of the Soviet Union, which was like someone unbuckling his sword. He was the last real Communist in Russia and it was said of him at that time that "A righteous man is departing."

The first concrete evidence of the success of the Reds' spring offensive was the forcing back of the southern wing of the White Army to the Belaya. That is a river that drains into the Volga, flowing north to south in the section mentioned here, aside from its meanderings, and then is joined by the Dioma and the Ufa at Ufa. Its direction changes just before that, at the mouth of the Sim. The city of Ufa, on the railroad, quite naturally formed the fulcrum of the White front, which stretched off to the north and south from either side of the great east-west railway line. One should not be deceived by the expression "front," however. The Russian Civil War was neither purely a war of mobility and separate groups – and perhaps least of all at the stage under consideration here – nor should one think in terms of the continuous, fortified entrenchments of the preceding World War. There was a front line. But it was constantly full of gaps, coming apart here, being stabilized there. Hence the many encircling manuevers, hence perhaps also the increasing importance of the cavalry, which would actually prove to be decisive in the Polish campaign in the following year. The miserable roads virtually excluded the rapid shifting of troops by truck – and there were no trucks to be had anyway. The Civil War and the Red "war of liberation" were clearly – as far as the application of technical means was concerned – far below the level of the World War. It was, in part, a matter of making do with remnants, since the war industries were already as good as silent. This paucity of weapons was especially prominent in the Red Army, while the Whites were actually receiving, ever since the onset of the intervention by the Entente, the necessary war materials in increasing amounts.

And so, in May the Whites' retreat from west to east in the southern sector of the front began in the direction from Bugrulan to Sterlitamak, which lay on the western shore of the Belaya. About May twenty-third, positions were taken up on the west bank, positions that were unfavorable and could not possibly be held for long, since there one had the river at one's back. Because of that withdrawal on the southern flank, a gap formed at Ufa, and a rather broad one at that. Trotsky immediately set in motion an offensive thrust in the direction of Birsk (on the Belaya north of Ufa). This was supposed to be contained by the Third Ural Corps and the 11th Division which would then go over to the counterattack. The counterattack, initially successful, came to a halt. The troops were withdrawn toward Ufa once again and then, along the entire extent of the front, beyond the Belaya.

To the south of the city of Ufa stood the best elements of the White Army, Russian troops under the command of General Kappel, a corps which later was to attain a grisly reputation.

Trotsky pressed after them to bring about a decisive conclusion to the campaign. The battle for Ufa lasted only a short while. The conclusion was provided by the mutiny of an entire regiment of the Ural Division – they killed their officers and resolutely went over to the Reds. On June 8, the Fifth Soviet Army marched into Ufa. A thrust attempted soon thereafter by General Gajda in the northern sector, in the area Solikamsk-Glasov-Perm, had no lasting success, ending in what amounted to a retreat. Gajda, who at that point had command of the Russian troops as well, had to relinquish that command as the result of a falling out with Kolchak. The significance of the Czechs began to diminish on the whole after the collapse of their efforts on the Volga. In the north there was a general withdrawal from that point as well and with that occurred a decisive event: the major northern east-west railroad line through the Urals, between Perm and Ekaterinburg, fell into the hands of the Reds and, as a result, also the junction points of the connecting lines that ran to the south along both sides of the Urals to join the major southern east-west line Ufa-Zlatoust-Cheliabinsk. The Whites were thus cut off from their rail connections with the north. The Northern Urals are lower and here the Red troops moved forward more easily. That is the only explanation for the otherwise incomprehensible fact that Trotsky needed scarcely four weeks to force his way across the Urals at Zlatoust; indeed, after this period of time had already firmly extablished himself on the Asiatic side. Anyone familiar with those areas (particularly, a battle-tested front-line soldier) and can visualize possibilities for defensive positions would quickly be convinced that, in the area of the southern railroad line near Zlatoust, with its gorges and natural rock fortifications, he could hold off a more numerous enemy for a good, long time with a few groups of men and machine guns properly deployed here and there, as long as they had some food and water in their packs and particularly if the opponent were poorly supplied with artillery, which was the case with the Reds at that time. But none of that counted for much at that point – the enemy had already advanced so far in the north that it would not take much for him to to be able to attack from behind. So when the Whites withdrew to the mountain passes of the Urals after the penetration of their front at Ufa, this could not be regarded, in view of their reversals in the north, as a stabilization but merely a way-station. The barrier of the Urals was unable to hold back the Red thrust against Siberia, no matter how splendidly they were suited for that by nature, because the Whites withdrew into the area with an already totally irregular front. For that, Gajda no doubt bore part of the responsibility because of his failed counterattack on the northern sector of the front. During the first days of July, the Fifth Soviet Army occipied Cheliabinsk, the first railroad station on the Asiatic side; that very city which had been taken by the Czechs on the night of May 25, 1918 now signaled the beginning of the Whites' collapse in Eastern Russia and Siberia.

After the capture of Cheliabinsk, some 700 kilometers of flat country still separated the Soviet troops from Omsk, the seat of the Kolchak government and the foreign missions.The advance was made more difficult by the fact that the retreating Whites often blew up the water towers, so that at times the railroad became unusable in the steppe regions, quite aside from the dynamiting of the river bridges (over the Tobol at Kurgan, which at that location had a rather insignificant size for Siberian rivers, and again over the Ishim at Petropavlovsk). Indeed, the retreat soon assumed the character of a rout in that sector. The figures speak quite clearly: to take the section of railway as far as Omsk (700 kilometers) the Fifth Army needed only four months after the fall of Cheliabinsk, since Omsk itself fell on November 15th. Thereafter, however, this advance increased to an entirely different pace: the stretch from Omsk to Krasnoyarsk amounts to around 1250 kilometers and was taken by the Fifth Army in two months. From there to Irkutsk is another 1000 kilometers, which only took four more weeks. Into the unspeakable misery of the completely disorganized withdrawal from Omsk slashed the Siberian winter with a fierceness even more terrible than that of the enemy. With unbridled brutality the foreigners, especially the Czechs, took over the rolling stock of the railroads. No one worried about Kolchak anymore. Even he was rolling toward the east somewhere among the endless columns of Czechs. Nevertheless, during the evacuation of Omsk, he and his detachment succeeded in loading onto his train and taking along the entire Russian gold reserves that had been dragged along from Europe by the Whites. Even these 10,000 puds (1 pud = 35 pounds) were later, in Irkutsk, to fall into the hands of the Reds, along with their protectors.

About the same time as the crossing of the Urals there was heavy fighting on another, quite distant front, namely at Iamburg, east of Petrograd. There the Reds succeeded in beating the English, with the capture of many English officers, thus thwarting General Iudenich's offensive against St. Petersburg. About the same time as the fall of Omsk, however, the sizable forces of General Denikin were defeated in the Ukraine, so that they had to evacuate Kiev. In fact, the breakthrough at Ufa defines the turning point in the history of the liberation of Russia from the Entente and their vassals. Because from that time on, the Reds triumphed on every front. Yet to come, of course, was the English-French intervention in the Crimea, which is associated with the name of the Russian General Wrangel; still to be waged was the Polish campaign, which gloriously commemorates the Red Cavalry. However, ponderous destiny had already turned on its hinges.

Shortly after the breakthrough at Ufa, the terror began. Strung up on telegraph poles along the railway to be found by the advancing Red Army soldiers were people who had perhaps failed to conceal their joy over the advance. Such murders were not the result of some conviction or other; such murders were more likely carried out by hands that were themselves already chilled by the anguish of death, that did their work hastily and convulsively in order to warm themselves one last time in the lust of still- held power. By late summer and early autumn, the dissolution of the White units was already beginning to spread more and more rapidly. The gigantic, exhausting distances loosened the marching order of the fighting units, pulled them apart, and easily delivered the isolated, delayed, individual detachments into the hands of their enemies. Or, on the other hand . . . some just stayed where they were, left their units and disappeared into the forest or hid in a village, or deserted in a band and pillaged and burned, brutally and hopelessly, until the rifles of the peasant partisans or a regular Red Army detachment put an end to specter and danse macabre – provided, of course, that they had not already been shot by one of their own officers.

Untouched by the raging terror were the already autumnally bare birch woods – white trunks trailing off a thousandfold, a silver keyboard for sunbeams. Light from the pale sky falls through the expanded spaces between defoliated branches. Perhaps a cut-off patrol stumbles in there with the enemy or hunger on their heels and their brains losing their grip in the incipient fear of death . . . there stands a bush on the edge of the forest, leaf after leaf resignedly losing hold, floating to the ground. Beyond lies the steppe, completely clear. To one marching along in the woods and looking out onto its undulating hills or out toward its distant edge, things appear different from every clearing or cut-over area, different from each vaulted, still-leafy passageway, and from the spaces between trunks and branches that open out or close down upon themselves. Out there, however, the eye often plunges into a veritable, real war, into the beginning of a great battle, whose sudden, yellow bursts of shrapnel hang in the air, alien to the landscape and sky and therefore immediately arresting. And now shot after shot can already be heard and one feels the air being lashed by the bullets' passage. But if one were way over there, in lightness and peace, right at the exact opposite side of the steppe, where the edge of heaven sits down upon the earth, so unthreatening, dreamy, and distant that one could well imagine the family house there . . . the larger-than-life, overly close center of gravity of a still somewhat hazy and indistinct childhood world, the starting point, the launching point of all those boyish longings that obstinately sense their true dwelling place at the very opposite edge of the city . . . it must be bright over there, related to the bright green of spring, glowing with newness. And nevertheless, though scarcely comprehensible, though beyond the field of vision, as near as nothing else in the world . . .

Stangeler awakened, opened eyes stuck together, and looked at the three empty beds in this room of the convalescent ward. He himself was lying in the fourth bed. Outside the window stood trees with their foliage already thinned out by fall; beyond that was a clear view across the river.

A new nurse walked in. The uniform, the whiteness, the cap – all of that at first caused Stangeler to repress recognition. Only when she bent over him, looked at the chart above his head, and asked "How are you?" in German did he realize that she was that friend of Alwersik's who'd walked along the quay with him and Jan back then during the summer.

He wanted to go on dozing – he had scarcely emerged from his half-slumber. Now there was something there, in his imagination – the evening dress of an elegant woman, in fact. But he couldn't associate it with anything and, much as he was used to rooting around in his mind, this time he was just too lazy.

But suddenly he was excited by the absolute certainty that he had previously completely separated two things that belonged together: first, there was the quay and the balmy summer evening and that thoughtful, melancholy-repulsive conversation . . . second, sometime or other up on the Sopka he had stepped into a fire, absent-minded, dull, tired. Both things also belonged together with a certain familiar story of Dorian's . . . and the evening gown belonged to it as well!

He tried to sit up suddenly, but his bandages pulled. The tiny pain had the effect of a chemical that causes a precipitation in a cloudy solution and makes it clear. And so there were threads other than his own back-and-forth, threads about which he knew nothing at all? Hah!

With the impetuous and innocent joy in thinking that was in keeping with his youth, he threw himself into trying to sort out the confusion. His capacity for thinking, well-developed through years of practice, now, for the first time in his life, came up against other people and external circumstances; but accustomed to hard work in the dimness of his own inner life, he succeeded here, faced with obvious facts, in arriving at conclusions with lightning speed.

However, Stangeler did not swell up with exaggerated self-importance, as might have bespoken his nature; he swallowed hard and didn't say a word to Katia. Besides she didn't recognize him, it seemed – at least she did nothing to suggest it. He merely sent a note to Dorian at the camp asking him to come and visit, nothing more. Stangeler wanted to put his conclusions to the test.

The peasants' guerilla war against Kolchak and the Czechs in the forest around Minusinsk intensified more and more with the approach of winter. With increasing frequency, the bands broke out of their forest strongholds, penetrated further north into the valleys and gorges, causing unrest, and sent their undetected scouts even as far as the city of Krasnoyarsk, right up to the camp of their enemies. The branch line from Minusinsk to Achinsk in the southeast was still being held by the Czechs with difficulty, but they were unable to accomplish anything more there. And while the Red front flowed onward from the west like a ribbon of fire, while debris from exploding bridges flew high into the air behind Kolchak's retreating or halted convoys, their opponent managed, in the end, to achieve contact with the insurgents in the south, literally growing another limb, another arm with which to encircle Kolchak. Above all, however, a constant stream of valuable intelligence had already started to flow from the south.

As Dorian walked out of the gate of the camp, the clear distance of the landscape lay painfully across his breast like a counterpoise to his own distress. He had brought the latter with him, intensified a hundredfold, from out there, a terrible gift: that despairingly thrown-up arch of longing, temporarily barely quieted, rose out of him anew, at one time pure and clear as glowing, molten glass, at other times roaring off in a tempest of high waves and debris. How dear to the heart were leaf, grass, and tree, after you'd recognized them as companions from back there on the other side who'd come along over here, just as this earth here ran on from his feet to her feet, which were standing on it somewhere off in the distance, far behind the sharp edges of the hills out there, along whose contours the sky formed a border of even paler blue.

He carried her picture against his breast. How often it had been buried in his trunk in desperation, but always taken out again.

Could she then . . . step down upon this earth? This lay beyond any thought, an impossibility, even if an angel were to carry her over here, an impossibility even for an angel. The air's different, despite all, the buildings made of brick . . .

In a sparkling shell, ringing with pain, stood all that was past. Here, however, mightily encompassed, the gigantic whirlpool of the landscape, coiled gray-green from mountain to steppe to river.

He came down the steps, sat on the edge of Stangeler's bed. Then Katia walked in.

Don't think he didn't recognize her immediately; she had actually not changed a bit. He did recognize her immediately, or, better said, the moment the door opened. And she him.

She folded her hands. But at that moment he felt a sense of guilt and inadequacy within himself and realized transiently that something very difficult was going on there; and so he tore the picture from his shirt and held it out toward her.

Stangeler lay there half propped up, as well as he could; he was burning with curiosity – it really seemed as if he had taken the trick.

Dorian awakened, as he had almost always in the last half-year, from dreams that left a tender after-effect that bordered on tears. Then the outside world tore through the veil of sleep and entered with broad, firm steps: the brick wall of the barracks over there in the morning sun or the gloomy daylight . . . so he really was there in Siberia, from which there was no way back (home!) at all; but each morning upon awakening, this fact and knowledge attached itself straightaway to the situation in which he found himself: she's here. To be sure, he dreamed on in the same way as before and experienced each morning as always – that already quite familiar and sobering disappointment – but that he experienced in the invariable pause between his awakening and when the thought leaped out: she's really here!

Now he was down there every day. She had helped him through the intricacies involved in obtaining a long-term pass to and from the camp. Every morning now, he took the half-hour walk down. He was getting accustomed to unencumbered walking out in the open again. Every morning now he was actually in a hurry.

By now such haste was already a slight compulsion, because the walk was getting to be a pleasure for him, he would like to have prolonged it, to have turned off from the road and gone nowhere in particular. For him, it was only now beginning to be fall; only now was the hazy veil of that sorrow-filled summer falling away from him, only now was the distance becoming clear and nearby things sharp, now that this landscape no longer simply lay across his breast like a counterpoise to his distress, avoided by his tired senses. Unfettered at last, however, they stormed out through their gates, borne by a feeling of happiness, which they, now liberated and relieved of torment, soon impetuously left behind and forgot again. Dorian's body had been cleansed deep within, this natural union with the young woman had swept away that heavy, dull sadness that had trickled into his very fiber, tenacious, burdensome. For him, it was only now beginnng to be fall, even though the snow-laden air of winter already seemed to be hovering threateningly above the sharp contours of the hills everywhere, even though the landscape seemed to be awaiting the first storm's trumpet blare in the absolute silence. But how he seemed to hesitate despite all that! Somewhere over there behind the contours of the hills still lay some holy piece of ground where he had, up until just now, believed her to be, standing on the same earth as he was here. Still coming from over there, sweetly, in the gray of the waning evening, from the farthest corner of the landscape where the lights of the station are twinkling, unfettered dreams draw near to the sound of pipes.

In the course of their evening conversations, the three of them – Stangeler, Dorian, and Katia – soon brought up everything that concerned Alwersik and his conduct – which was, indeed, quite transparent. With Katia, Dorian often tried to talk about earlier times; he took the situation to mean, more or less, that they both had to return to the ground that had once been common to them, that had to be holy to them, in other words. But all the while, she evaded him in her vague way. She embraced him, she pressed against him as if she were seeking shelter in his presence, or at any rate, in the present. For her, the Dorian of now had nothing to do with the Dorian of then and something completely new, without a past, seemed to have begun for her. Now and again she talked about Poccal, her husband, her good, ample mother, as she called him and was full of self-reproach to the point of tears and said she'd regretted everything so bittlerly after Alwersik's disappearance "and now you're here," she said and kissed Dorian "and I had nothing but good resolutions."

But within him everything was changing and behind the altered and expanded landscape, it all arranged itself neatly all the way back to the other side – whether it was the self-experienced, deep, and serious pain of the boy over a broken, little whip, or all the bright remnants from those days which were hanging dispersed within him, but now flowed together and were kneaded and squeezed, or the good feeling you had standing in front of the sink trying to make a usable ball of soap from all those left-over pieces and succeeded, happily enough, with the softening warmth of the water and the superior pressure of the kneading hands that pressed in all the protruding corners and smoothed them out and made them disappear . . .

Thus he lost himself in those images drifting in the half-light and shrank back from the alien touch of her words whenever she spoke about the troubles in which they found themselves or about her frequent, wild fears. Because then he recognized with guilt and horror that there was no secure resting place within him any longer for this pairing-off, this alliance that had developed. He no longer spoke much with her, and then only with lapses. She herself often spoke in quite general terms, such as, "I really think that all of you have lost a lot of your resolve and your ability to make decisions after living in the prison camp all these years, in other words, you don't have much left of that masculinity, I mean, just to stand there relaxed and unconcerned in life, always ready for something else, ready to go on rowing your boat wherever – you've lost that, right? That something that makes you strong, courageous, a real benefit to other people . . ."

She fell silent, her gaze dissolved, she was no longer looking outside, no longer at Dorian.

A few days later the first snow fell. But the wind remained calm.

Dorian stood in the central square of the camp, breathing deeply; the dizzying myriad of individual flakes rolled down into his field of vision. He had come from the camp office. He had just registered for the convoy of prisoners that was to leave for the east in a very few days, because the Krasnoyarsk camp was already being vacated. Close by, the horizon was already ablaze. At first, probably only those who volunteered would be transferred. The majority of the camp's inmates, however, were expecting salvation, freedom, and the possibility of going home at the hands of the approaching Red force.

That evening, Dorian went to Katia. In the rising wind of the first winter storm, the windows were rattling and the door blew open from the draft that accompanied him as he walked into her room. He said nothing to Katia about his intentions. They drank tea in the already deepening dusk, warm and snuggled together in the light of a small candle.

Out there where the ridges of the hills wander off, hurrying away in a veil of driving snow, out there, that which had to come is taking place on a broad panorama, gigantic and quite separate from the individual caught up in his own misery. Quick as lightning, hundreds slip from the backs of their horses, run on ahead, throw themselves to the ground and lie there with their shoulders tense, sending off volleys of sudden, snarling clouds from the barrels of their rifles. The smoke hangs over the landscape between the firing lines and mixes, drifting and sinking, with the banners of snow that blow over from the hilltops, mixes, finally, with the leaden gray distances in which lies the glow of burning villages, red and suppressed.

Stangeler slept for the last time in the hospital. He had been discharged, was to go back up to the camp on the following day. Was it some sort of recurrent fever or the sign of fully recovered health that his entire body seemed to him to be cracking and creaking in its seams, so to speak, as if some sort of partitions within him were giving way, as if his blood had found its way into new, broader passageways? Continually bubbling forth from a hidden spring, it forced its way out, climbed uneasily as if in dark gorges and valleys, and then sent its first, bold – even if still thin – trickles and rivulets right up to the very camp of the enemy, against whom an attack could not yet be attempted . . .

Here and there the peasants were beginning to break out of the forests to the south and into the open countryside, falling upon larger Czech detachments, slaughtering and murdering in the name of a justice which they considered to be – without asking themselves too many questions – assured. Indeed, whoever was fighting on the Red side had the feeling then that they were close to breaking through the last wall, that they were not only – as they had been half a year previously – as strong as the enemy, in other words, capable of putting the planned campaign into execution, of opposing him sucessfully, meeting him head-on – no, no, they were already close to completely repairing the destructive split in the empire, bringing it together for the future peace, whose work already beckoned and which would finally make it possible to leave their narrow preoccupation. Because, while they were still fighting with the old desperation and bitterness, still busying their bloody hands with the next task at hand, they had completely failed to notice that the deep red, suppressed glow on the horizon was gradually growing pale and that beyond the edges of the hills a new dawn was breaking, whose peaceful horns were about to proclaim that victory had, in complete silence, come full turn. Looking up, one sees, with deep astonishment, the bitterest adversary bowed down and tamed and above his shoulders one's gaze extends out into the brightening distance. The war or Kerensky, or the gigantic distance from here to Peking, or whatever is happening out there in all its many variations and here the little table in front of the bed, with sheets of paper on it; and, oh, all the haze and the shafts of light from receding masses of time full of strange figures and candles and full of ponds of sadness. Here, deep within, however, bubbling forth from deep springs are those rivulets, separated up till now, climbing as if through dark gorges and valleys, forcing their unsettling way upward. But in the end they all whirl around and run together together, as if into a sphere without edges or clefts, gigantic, glowing and clearly discernible, so that perhaps one can also see clearly that mountain range of war made of rubble and human bodies that extends darkly from west to east, making the entire horizon flame up dark red. Yes, even that gets tossed in too! Because the edge of the ancient forest and its ravines has now been reached, one's gaze easily traverses the undulations of gentler hills, the rider shades his eyes with his hand and strains – off in the distance lies the city. Then that is the direction to proceed on foot after dark has fallen, in order to steal in . . .

The wind that blows. The blood that stands still in the room. This portion of the world in a seed, in our breast, we scarcely discern it: in here and out there. But the body has windows out of which we fall and has gates and dreams – things pour in, mixing together . . .

A loud bang on the door made Dorian and Katia suddenly jump apart. "Hide!" she hissed, "maybe it's a patrol." But the door had already sprung open, a burst of cold air poured in from outside, mixing with the warmth inside . . . a soldier's fur coat could be seen, a red stubblebeard – Alwersik. “O boye – Oh God,” she groaned and folded her hands. Alwersik closed the door behind him. “Well,” he said, “here I am and . . . there you two are happily together . . .” A bitter expression crept into Katia's face. “Where've you come from? Such craziness! Yes, yes, I understand all right . . . no doubt you have things to talk about, you two! . . . well?..I'm leaving, I'll go make some tea,” and she was already in the next room. Alwersik threw his coat on the floor and let himself down somewhat heavily. Dorian felt these moments coiling around him, but at the same time possibly bringing a simple solution. He came right out with it, told him everything, saying that he was leaving in three days with the convoy. “That way's good,” Jan agreed. “We won't say anything to her, you just leave and don't come back. I need her now . . . as a base. I've come from the south, I'm a scout, do you understand? I'll be coming and going three or four times and I want to spend several days living and sleeping here in her house. She needs to provide cover for me, otherwise it won't work. It's good that you're leaving, Dorian, things are going to get bad here. Do you know how things stand with the Whites? Matter of fact, things don't stand anymore, it's all over. In six weeks, we'll be here . . . What do you know about Stangeler? . . . Is that right? . . . In the hospital until just recently? Yes, OK, we don't need to try to fool each other, Dorian. Damn, a lot of things have changed.” Katia walked in.

Things went on like that for several weeks. He came, stayed awhile, and disappeared again. She trembled with fear. For the first few days, she kept asking about Dorian. Then he finally told her that he had already left. "You bastards!" she screamed, "what are you doing to me? You bastards, back and forth . . . I'm just being handed on from one to the other!" she howled. He simply pushed her onto the bed, turned her over, laughed, and took her. As she felt him deep within her very fiber, as if she were bringing that man there into the world like some kind of giant child, things swam, foreign and distant, through her imagination – a genuine, antique Russian tea service, vivid crimson, with a sugar bowl of wild, barbarian shape with brick-red zigzags . . . she suddenly shivered with horror and groaned.

Each time he came he brought a rucksack heavy with supplies, often a lot of money as well, not only bundles of the increasingly worthless Kolchak banknotes, but hard currency as well, dollars, francs, even gold. He kept at her until she gave up her job as an aide in the hospital, managing to convince her that sooner or later she'd be sent to help out in one of the typhus barracks that were quickly filling up as the winter went on. She was currently receiving the officer's salary of her husband, whose whereabouts was unknown to the military authorities; he was listed as missing.

A few days before Christmas in the "new style," that is, on the twentieth of December, Jan turned up at midnight, once again carrying a heavy load, and said he was going to stay awhile. With that, he crept into his corner of the bedstead and remained lying there, eating and sleeping, day in day out; it seemed as if he were belatedly satisfying the months of sleep deprivation and ravenous hunger, and he only got up to stretch and loll about in a huge, wooden tub full of hot water. She was completely drawn into this life, since even her own customary, taxing work was being increasingly neglected. He had her buy up whatever good things were left at the market. He even showed up one night disguised in a peasant jacket and set down a ridiculously heavy rucksack full of white flour, lard, tea, and sugar. She stared at his face as he slept, and the bulldog-like compactness of his features put her into a rage – even the way his jaw muscles squeezed together! "You dirty dog, what are you up to?" she thought, "What's going on in your head? Do you imagine that maybe I'm a sack of flour, too, or a pot of lard, or something else useful?" But when he awakened and – he did it every time – reached for her immediately, her legs flew despite all that and she threw herself upon him. He squinted at her through his half closed lids and his look told her each time that he knew very well how things stood here and that his life was, to a certain extent, in her hands. But at the same time there lay in his look the repulsive hint that she was now under the same blanket as he was, that she was already involved whether she liked it or not. Aside from that he was extraordinarily tender and warm toward her, indeed, his tenderness was like a flood, almost numbing and debilitating. But she convulsed with hatred – which almost immediately sank back powerless again – whenever she sensed or considered what cunning calculation lay behind even that. It often seemed to her that he was watching her, even when his eyes were closed. Like a cat, he lay rolled up there in his corner, but at other times he did all sorts of incomprehensible things like drawing for hours or writing page after page.

And so they lived, constantly as if in deep twilight, always in the company of the bubbling samovar, pressed together for hours in the light of a small candle, while outside the winter hurled the thundering masses of its storms against the houses and, in the very next moment, was already surpassing the blare of its trumpets with ten thousand new trumpets. It was precisely during such wild rushes of wind that she would suddenly feel – and it seemed to her as if she were about to go crazy and start raving – the pitiless, inexorable, and already completely unbearable quality of her entire situation. Her stomach was heavy, Jan ate constantly and stuffed her full as well, her mind was dull, her temples pounded. But what irritated her most about him was a certain satisfied waiting, that expressed itself more and more shamelessly, a certain confidence that seemed to say that he knew full well why he was lying around here eating and grooming himself – because everything was going just fine, all you had to do was wait just a little longer.

Christmas was past, New Year's as well, it may have been the fourth or fifth of January when all of this just sort of exploded out of her one evening and she tried desperately to put it into words with Jan. She gave a political speech. He merely grunted. She shifted over to personal accusations. He picked up his fur and walked backwards through the door and out into the drift-covered garden and breathed in the fresh air. Then he came back in, strolled through the room and caressed her breast in passing.

She suddenly bit his hand with all her strength. He

laughed and pushed her away. He was standing with his back to the street, in front of the closed shutters. As if something had suddenly dawned on her, she rushed over to the bedstead and pulled his pistol from beneath the pillows. Her face twitched with spasms of frenzy, she felt ice cold, she was trembling throughout her whole body, her shoulders jerking up and down. At that moment, shots were heard, far away, one, two, six, then salvos, then tatatatatatatat . . .

A machine gun. "What's that?" she screamed. "That's us!" he bellowed and laughed as he threw open the shutters. The cold made a haze as it poured in. "Dog! Dog!" she screeched, "you Red dog . . ." and now her hand jerked up . . . crack, crack, crack . . . but he was already through the window. She rushed out, shooting at him as he ran down the alley, enraged, shooting until the empty breech clicked open. At the end of the alley, groups men went running by, now the rifle fire was quite close. And then . . . wwummm. Field artillery.

Alwersik was wrong. Neither the peasants from the south nor the Red Army coming from the west had reached Krasnoyarsk. A local revolt, instigated by the workers at the railroad repair shops, brought about the fall of the city which was the destination of Kolchak's retreating army, the mirage that promised rest and relief from hunger and cold. Man for man, some lying frozen and sick on the transport sleds, the others marching four by four – the only forms of mobility left to the army now that the railroad lines were totally blocked – man for man they dreamed of a roof over their heads and the provisions that had to be there in the Krasnoyarsk barracks and in the city as well.

These approaching masses now saw themselves faced by the revolutionary workers' council following the coup d'etat. And they now wanted to hold the city at all costs, had no intention of surrendering it to those hordes of soldiers.

At that point the cold had become frightful again – on New Year's Day it had still been relatively warm. On January 5, skirmishes began with the Cossacks who formed the advance guard of the Whites. On January 7, the head of the army became visible, dragging itself along out on the steppe behind the barracks area and the prisoner of war camp – a circumscribed, gray something that was pushing its way onto the background color of the snow. The armed workers occupied the northern edge of the camp – they even had a few machine guns as well, but on the whole their strength was not great. The roofs of the barracks situated to the north were black with curious war prisoners who were squatting there in swarms and clusters hoping to get a view. In addition, there were some people in the camp who took things as seriously as they actually were. The workers soon opened fire, more or less from the middle of the crowd of prisoners, who, for that reason, were sure to be massacred in the event of a White victory. The gray army-worm out there crept across the steppe, always at the same distance from the edge of camp, where there had always been trenches and barbed wire. It was nearly quiet out there; the whole thing made a rather pitiful impression. The workers were now shooting like crazy, at a distance of perhaps 1,500 paces. The indifference of those being shot at in that way had a strange and horrifying effect. Only now and then did a bullet whistle over from out there.

Through the half-empty barracks of the enlisted men ran two workers' leaders and an Austrian lieutenant, a former teacher at the Wiener-Neustadt military academy. Men gathered around him; somehow the word had even made it up to the roofs and people started to squirm down in clusters. Then the officer spoke, twenty words, and the situation was clear to everyone. During the short speech, noises could be heard – spak-spak-spak, then suddenly countless bullets were smashing into the wood. They were coming from out there, now the battle had really begun. Hasty, heavy rattling of wagons right afterward. Now things were happening quickly. The men – predominately Viennese and other Austrians, with a few groups of Imperial Germans and Hungarians thrown in – the Poles and Czechs having pulled everyone else back – those men charged out of the barracks with lightning speed and organized themselves in the cover of one of the larger brick buildings. There may have been a hundred of them or so, the voice of the short lieutenant somehere in their midst. As they ran by, each man was handed a rifle and cartridge belt by the workers who brought up wagon after wagon full of weapons. It all went unbelievably swiftly. The troops left the camp from the east side, formed a long, drawn-out skirmish line, and launched a properly organized infantry attack. The field gun that had been taken by the workers on the night of the putsch was wheeled up to support them.

And so it happened in that winter of 1920, with its glittering snow and numbing cold, with its sunny, shining prospects that rose from the landscape here and there – it happened that the flowing waves of the steppe, the flanks of the hills, and the ice on the river all seemed to be covered with countless, dark spots – the runaway sleigh horses of the largely decimated White army. They were falling over by the hundreds from hunger and cold. The best ones were picked out by the peasants, but almost all the animals had been driven to exhaustion, were crippled, or covered with sores from their harnesses. The danger that might emerge from these countless cadavers with the approach of spring was still confined by the cold to flesh frozen hard as bone. However, the local Soviet had already ordered the Austrian engineers to dynamite and excavate a huge rectangular pit. Into it proceeded, loaded on wagons or dragged with ropes, a veritable stream of the fellowship of four-footed sufferers, finally come to rest there.

A few days after the already-mentioned battle, the Fifth Soviet Army marched into the city by divisions, but it was just a brief stopover, although the staff stayed for a longer time. Of the Russian part of the White Army, the only intact and battle-worthy group at that point was General Kappel's Volga Corps, which was joined here and there by the few isolated units that had remained together. This Kappel division was now about 12,000 strong. At temperatures of thirty below zero, they fought their way through to the east intact, dealing bloody blows to the pursuing Reds, partisan bands, and rebellious Irkutsk troops, completely plundering all the towns that lay in their path, and torturing hundreds of peasants to death. That memorable and terrible march of the Kappel division has often been referred to as the "ice campaign," during which the group itself gradually became smaller, more from typhus, hunger, and cold than from losses in battle. But what remained were tested, battle-hardened men who had been fighting for the better part of two years and who would surrender to no one. It is characteristic that, during the heavy fighting between the Kappel division and the Irkutsk forces, no prisoners were taken by either side. In the main, the Volga Corps succeded in making their way, in closed formation, past Irkutsk and Lake Baikal to Verkhne-Udinsk and then on to Chita. To be sure, in the Transbaikal, they enjoyed the support of the Cossack chieftan Semenov, who still occupied the area. In Irkutsk the Kolchak regime had already been toppled at the beginning of January by a revolution. In the beginning, the "Social Revolutionaries" (Mensheviks) – in other words a group that already stood somewhat to the right – had been involved, but the supporters of the Soviets very quickly succeeded in displacing the former and seizing and exercising power themselves. From that point on, the Kolchak government no longer existed. The French General Janin, together with the foreign military missions, Japanese troops, and whoever else was still in Irkutsk, all gradually withdrew in whatever way they could. The Czechs had already surrendered their valuable pawn. Even before the Irkutsk revolt had assumed a purely Bolshevik character, Kolchak had been turned over by them to the new local government, the so-called "Political Center." The representative of the Entente powers had agreed forthwith. And so Kolchak was allowed to fall as easily as Wrangel was somewhat later. At that point, the citizens of Irkutsk were negotiating with the Fifth Army to curtail its advance and recognize the not-yet-occupied territory as a more or less independent, democratic – in other words, not Bolshevik – republic, but of course nothing came of that. Be that as it may, having Kolchak in their custody meant a great advantage for Irkutsk during those negotiations. The Czechs were in no position to negotiate with the Reds directly and tried to use the new Irkutsk regime as their intermediary, and to improve their position, turned over Kolchak in return for safe passage for their convoys. When the Bolshevik Party very soon took the helm in Irkutsk, they naturally came into possession of the person of the "Regent," who was sitting in jail there. Then, when the Fifth Army attacked the last of the Czech convoys near Nizhne-Udinsk, about halfway between Krasnoyarsk and Irkutsk, and actually threatened the Czechs with destruction, the latter now turned to the Soviets who were in sole power in Irkutsk with the request that they intercede with the command of the Fifth Army to resume the prior negotiations regarding safe withdrawal. Directly afterward, however – as incomprehensible as it may seem – the Czechs were perfidious enough, despite their promise of neutrality, to suddenly attack the Irkutsk troops from the rear while they were involved in their heaviest fighting against the Kappel Division . . . Well, in all that confusion and considering the exhaustion that the Red troops had to contend with after their incredible advance, the staff of the Fifth Army obviously decided to close their eyes to certain events and on the sixth of January agreed, despite all, to grant the Czechs safe conduct to Vladivostok, together with their weapons and supplies – everyone was really just delighted to get those beasts out of the country as soon as possible and have one enemy less.

The Irkutsk Reds brought Kolchak to trial. He was, after the agreement of the Fifth Army had been obtained, shot on the morning of February 7.

The Czechs had simply deserted their comrades in the Polish Legion, whose convoys were moving by rail directly behind them, had not made mention of them at all in the treaty which they had just concluded without the Poles' knowledge. Even if the withdrawing Czechs still suffered a good deal of violence, even if the Siberian peasants, whenever they came upon isolated groups of Czech legionnaires, looked for the nearest tree and reached for the nearest rope to take revenge, late though it might be, on their bloodthirsty, foreign tormentors – still and all, the fate of the Czechs in Siberia was considerably more merciful than that of the Poles. Because the latter fell into their enemies' hands lock, stock, and barrel; everything was taken from them, not only their weapons, but also their uniforms and all their warm clothing, in return for which they received miserable rags for the forced march back to Krasnoyarsk, where they were penned up in barracks until the last bit of work could be squeezed out of their frozen and half starved bodies. Those who reported sick were simply beaten to death by the Red overseers. The officers of the Polish Legion, some of whom had already been captured during the retreat from Cheliabinsk to Omsk, were court-martialed and shot without exception, for abusing their soldiers, spying, and for counterrevolutionary activities in general.

The course of further events in the Transbaikal and off in the far east soon became slower, more gradual, and less cohesive. One must recall that about this time the campaign against Wrangel to the west and the more extensive Polish war were beginning. The Red troops extended their advance to the east in a different fashion from previously; that spring they even allowed the formation of a "Republic of the Far East," whose leaders made their way to Verkhne-Udinsk, some 300 kilometers to the east of Irkutsk. At the head of this buffer state stood a man who had been imprisoned in Irkutsk during Kolchak's regime, Krasnoshtshokov, the very same man who had negotiated, as one of the Irkutsk delegates, for the establishment of such a republic. Three hundred kilometers further to the east in Chita, the Whites had established themselves, namely the Kappel Division together with the men of the Cossack Semenov. In Vladivostok, a more or less thrown-together coalition ruled, a political stillbirth that was swept away by the Japanese in short order. Here were concentrated, as well, the troops of the Entente, insofar as they had not already been evacuated by ship. In the following days, the Japanese even succeeded in temporarily occupying large parts of the coastal areas and the province of Amur. By November of 1920 the Whites had already been mopped up after the fighting forces of Semenov had been destroyed. Chita became the seat of the Republic of the Far East, which, for practical purposes, soon resembled the rest of Soviet Russia. The last White rearguard actions in the east were carried out by Baron Ungern-Sternberg, a wild Baltic adventurer of extraordinary bravery and great military talent. His insanely daring robber bands were finally finished off at the Chinese border in June of 1921, after the Chinese government itself had vainly sent troops against him. Ungern-Sternberg, who at one time had been in charge of the railroads for Semenov, ended his notable life in front of a Red firing squad.

For a very short time, the commandant of the Krasnoyarsk camp was that very Austrian lieutenant who had been the deciding factor in favor of the Reds during the battle on the steppe on the seventh of January. Additionally, a certain share in the favorable outcome was attributed, as it later turned out, to those prisoners who had not taken part in the battle. Probably the sight of their great numbers had had an inhibitory effect on the enemy. That Austrian officer then disappeared – where, no one knew – some even mentioned prison, others said he was commanding a unit in the east. And now he was superceded by one Hugo Blau, sent from the west with the rank of Brigadier. Rumor had it that he had already played a certain role in Siberia in 1918 and then, after the Czechs' loss of power, had escaped from a White prison and made his way to European Russia. Blau had obviously had quite a career.

There were now huge numbers of prisoners at Krasnoyarsk, packed into the cold barracks like cattle. The Germans and Austrians had to be taken out of their quarters and penned together to make room. All the officers lost their slightly more spacious lodgings. They were ten, even twenty to a room and in the end, the order came to leave the stone buildings entirely and move into the earthen barracks. Here they lived, in temperatures hardly more than a few degrees above zero and in darkness from four in the afternoon. Albert Lehnder came to see Stangeler – after years – in the belief that he was done for. "Here's where I found it," he said, opened his shirt and displayed his bushy chest. "Here! In nine days . . ." He meant a louse. The nine days referred to the interval during which typhus – should the bite have transmitted the germ – would develop. In this way Stangeler and Lehnder, who stood before him pale as a sheet, found each other again. Stangeler's face resembled a hard knot, his eyes stood on even more of a slant, his cheekbones stood out prominently. Almost everyone walked unsteadily and haltingly as a result of hunger; once a day there was stinking fish soup and a chunk of bread the size of a fist.

Sickness flared up. In Lehnder's room there were three cases; Stangeler's bunkmate died. All the misery, hunger, helplessness, and desolation seemed to want to melt together and perish quietly upon the giant fires of the fever that reached out, tossing piles of the sick onto the straw mattresses of the hospitals like so many stranded fish. A maw opened, into which thousands wandered. Corpses frozen stiff as boards – burning with fever just a few hours before, but now the clattering load on a cart, with a withered arm or leg sticking out – went tumbling into the huge, excavated rectangles of the mass graves, a fellowship of sufferers, finally come to rest here.

To the same extent that the Red attack, having swept across Krasnoyarsk and the Yenesei region, now proceeded further toward the east, events hurried along here as well and people were already moving in – with offices, authorities, commissions. The participation of the imprisoned Germans, Austrians, and Hungarians was considerable; many joined the army or found other ways to feather their nests. Those, however, who were still unable to adapt to things as they now were remained in a state of neutrality, hanging in the air, so to speak, and simply remained part of the masses; and soon realized that their one-time comrades were discovering those masses to be a suitable object for the exercise of their newly-won official status and their greater or lesser degrees of power. Out of the mud stirred up by events crept figures whom life would otherwise have hardly allowed to put in an appearance as significant individuals. Those "Comrades" Sandbank, Nascher, Fodor, Kiss, Gold, Powolny, and Traxlehner – who had they been previously? And where did he come from, that German, Sergeant Obst, who, as commandant of the entire Voyenny Gorodok, was now carrying on the reorganization and administration of the prison camp in accordance with his political convictions? It happened again and again that one, in fact, no longer knew how to behave on recognizing – in some military personage wearing a uniform with lots of red, who came into the camp to look things over – a Goldstaub or a Kiss. Indeed, they all carried "the flaming sign of the times" on their foreheads, namely, in the form of a flap of red cloth sewed onto their high fur caps, flaps of red cloth that were a lot bigger than prescribed, bigger than the ones worn by the soldiers of the Fifth Army fighting at the front. From the people mentioned, however, was formed the so-called "International Detachment."

Stangeler, who had been hanging around in the gateway to the municipal command post, was, to his surprise, suddenly addressed by Alwersik. The latter looked like he did formerly – neat, shaved. They walked somewhat off to the side together, in the direction of the quay. "What are you doing here?" asked Alwersik.

"Cultural department – the German daily newspaper – the German language art magazine that's supposed to be started, 'Via Nova.' I've been relieved of all other duties."

"Great – and how's it going?"

"Id – i – o – tic," said the slant-eyed one, separating the syllables. "How about you . . .?"

"I was in the south, with the peasants. Their leader. In the end, a scout. Now I'm commanding the local shock troops." The shock troops were a small, select detachment that had the job of immediately beating down any local counterrevolution that seemed about to erupt.

"So you're now a completely dependable man of the party," Stangeler said, grinning.

Suddenly Alwersik asked whether "the date" had already been set and Stangeler answered no.

It had become known that the Reds' intention was to once again allow all foreigners serving in the Red Army – all the "Internationals" in other words – to voluntarily muster out in order to be sent home after the transportation difficulties had been solved. Whoever remained in their army units after that date would be considered to have "dedicated his life to the Red cause and placed himself completely at its disposal" and any attempt of such a person to leave the Soviet zone of influence would be considered desertion, punishable by instant death. This measure sprang from the attempt to cleanse the foreign units and assure their loyalty.

"Do you realize that, as former officers, we're hardly likely to get sent home in the near future?" asked Stangeler. "Do you know that our turn comes at the very last? That's official!"

"I'm still gonna get out," snarled Alwersik angrily. "I've had enough. The whole thing's a fraud. I fought, I went along with it. A bunch of crap. I don't wanna be tied to this crap anymore. I'll get home on my own. If they catch me traveling apart from the convoys, the worst they'll do is lock me up, not bump me off for desertion. Besides, as a 'writer' here at headquarters, you've got to belong to some army unit, right? What're you going to do?"

"Get out,"answered Stangeler. "I can't stand it anymore, I can't wait any longer. I puke every day. For these stoneheads I've gotta dig passages out of the best authors – whether it's Strindberg or Dostoyevski – that fit in with their junk but were never, never even possibly, meant that way. So they can use them a quotes in their slimy editorials."

Scum and filth formed ahead of the revolution and at its edges. And even if its heart, that pure motivating force at its center around which everything revolved, held unwaveringly to a course directed toward a single, valid future – out there amidst the raging upheaval of events, this very same movement pushed or lifted hundreds and thousands of men out of their constraints, so that they fell by the wayside as their baser instincts began to assert themselves. A veritable hailstorm of uprooted, unbound individuals accompanied this developing new order out on its whirling periphery, carried along and dancing around it like countless tiny fragments or specks of dust, like a fog that softens contours, like cosmic dust around a new star. Of course, at the center, in the Red Kremlin at Moscow, one could stay focused on those contours, which could be seen better there, from the inside out. And at the same time, there, each bit of human individuality had been suppressed in advance and offset by the direction of their gaze which no longer seemed to comprehend the things of this earth that were near at hand, but only a distant horizon – not heaven, however, even if those eyes scarcely seemed to be earthly any longer. But they were just that. Earthly, as well, was the hand that with the dispassionate stroke of a pen crossed name after name from a list. Even the room in which that happened was of this earth, and the bell that was activated in some interior space sealed with a heavy, padded door – that was of human creation. It rang far outside in some office, from which a young man immediately hurried through the long, empty corridors. He received the orders that were to be distributed by the telegrapher, for the most part names of individuals with a cipher next to them. Thus the revolution began the hopeless task of cleansing itself; thus it attempted, from its core toward its edges, to gradually annihilate what it, itself, had once upon a time churned up into the light of day.

And with what a churning! And with what degree of confusion must those who had been thrown upward have arrived on top! Out of the cold, hunger, and gloom of the earthen barracks or out of the mines, then directly confronted by the possibility of helping a captured Czech captain to escape, with the flick of a wrist, so to speak, in a way completely free of risk – and in return for which, taking possession of his wife and those stable American dollars printed on paper like fabric. You warm room! You fine eats! You lighted room! You soft bed! The rapture of one who landed on top was not directed at mere lifeless things and the trappings of good luck; no, he worshiped them as divinities, the gods of life, the gods of joy. In a moment of decision, the fruits of which were no longer in question, the soul in many cases turned toward newly granted life with deep emotion and warmth, turned away from death with revulsion, indeed almost believing in this life and its happiness. And then it was just a matter of going forward on the same, warm pathway, whenever one got rid of an accomplice or possible informer or an enemy by means of a murder that could be carried out without risk in such varied, indirect ways – whether it be through political denunciation or something else in the name of the Revolution. Oh, and then you end up in front of the firing squad yourself, though you just wanted to live, nothing more. Yes, really, nothing more, in spite of that overly large red star on your cap.

But, along with the Red wave, some believed they could see a surge of brotherliness and freedom – salvation after Kolchak's terror. However, near an island downstream, not far from Krasnoyarsk, those holes had been hacked through the ice, those maws which swallowed alive anyone who displeased or ran afoul of those now in power. In the cellars of prisons, pistols murdered row after row of White officers and even their wives, while out on the streets or in the courtyards, trucks with their accelerators all the way down provided a hellish roar to drown out the sound of the shootings. And soon afterward, a load of silent freight was dumped onto them, still warm.

The date until which withdrawal from Red Army units was still open to the "Internationals" had finally been made known and only simultaneously with that had this possibility and offer been officially announced, rather belatedly, on the first of March; and by 6 o'clock in the evening of the fifteenth of the month, everyone was supposed to have decided. It was also stated that the announcement had been considerably delayed through the influence of certain cliques among the Internationals who felt the necessity of having the largest possible number in agreement – with regard to going home – and therefore wanted to limit the number of dropouts by shortening the time period.

Alwersik and Stangeler had both long since decided. The slant-eyed one was mustered out immediately, went looking for work, and ended up as a loader at a branch of the former Nobel Petroleum company. When these matters had been put in order, he went to the headquarters of the shock troops. Simultaneously, a soldier walked into Alwersik's room, saluted, handed the commander a small, folded letter which he pulled from his boot, then disappeared. "The date . . . you already know?"

"Yeh, of course . . . so now we're finally through with this crap and can get out." At the same time Jan was unfolding the letter:

"Jan, for the love of Christ, I implore you to help. You are the only one who can save us. My husband is here, safe and sound, among the Polish prisoners, I've even seen him. How happy I was and grateful to God, and today I realize that I belong to him alone, as if to a mother. How good everything could be – and now we're supposed to die? Help us! I was arrested then and am now sitting in the Tjurma, most certainly because of the shooting I did that night – one of the neighbors probably informed on me and said I was shooting at the Reds. What nonsense! Koloman is accused of mistreating soldiers or some such thing, as are all the Polish officers – they are all facing the worst. The soldier who is bringing you this letter is trustworthy, the poor devil used to be a day laborer at the harbor, lived in my neighborhood. I often gave presents to his children . . . so he is bringing you this letter secretly. Perhaps in the camp there are Austrian officers and soldiers from Novo-Nikolaevsk who could give testimony for Koloman. He was the commandant there in 1918, you know. I beseech you to find out if anyone among your comrades up in the prison camp was in Nicolaievsk during the summer of 1918. Of course the best thing would be favorable testimony from ordinary soldiers – there is no doubt that if you can find witnesses, they will all speak out on his behalf – he was really so good to the men. I implore you in particular for your help. I have heard that you are fairly high up. The first proceedings against Koloman and me are set for March 17. Blau will be chairman because it is still considered a court-martial; the matter is not going to be taken up by the special commission called the Assobenaya Kommmissia or 'Cheka,' which is perhaps good luck. Please come to see me if that's possible without revealing our relationship and please, please look after Koloman. But he must never, never learn about anything, swear to me! I will never say why I did the shooting that night, never. Now that I have him again all of my infidelity will be submerged, everything that I did – please understand me. I beseech you for all of that. Help me, I beg you, in the name of your own mother.

Katharina Poccal"

Alwersik handed Stangeler the letter, gave him a few brief words of explanation. They exchanged only a few more words after the slant-eyed one had read it, then parted. Stangeler went back up to camp immediately to collect witnesses. Alwersik, however, presented himself at Blau's office. There, as one who had served the cause well, he found a favorable reception and said a good deal about the character of the captain. The Brigadier and Commandant of the City revealed himself as sympathetic toward the fate of such a humane officer, to whom the members of the Red Guard previously imprisoned at Nicolaevsk, as he now realized, owed a large debt of gratitude. He immediately filled out a memorandum ordering that Poccal be relieved of all labor and provided with better quarters, and reassured Alwersik as well with regard to the outcome of Poccal's trial, which, unless new facts were to come to light, was merely to be looked upon as a formality as things now stood. With Blau's orders in his pocket, Alwersik went next to the barracks in which the captured Polish officers were housed. There, in the dim light, dampness, and the steam which rose from clothing drying on the stove, he found the captain. Poccal looked as if he'd suffered a great deal and obviously expected nothing good at the sight of a Red commissar. Alwersik immediately arranged for Poccal's transfer to one of the former officers' buildings of the camp where there was still an empty room – in other words something fairly comfortable. The captain found it difficult to take his leave of his comrades, for whom he felt sorry. Already some of them had been taken away from there for, as had been learned later, their last walk.

And now to Katia. Alwersik stormed across town behind thick clouds from his violent breathing, while the streets and squares were perceived by his eye only fleetingly and fragmentedly in the dusk of the evening. Here, now, in the "Tjurma," in the prison where he expected the worst, he was surprised and relieved; Katia was confined alone, and in addition, not in a cell but in an empty side room of the prison office, where she also carried out the secretarial duties. Her room was well heated. Perhaps all of this was the result of her connections in the town. Alwersik was left alone with her without even having to give an order to that effect.

But now, when he saw her again, as he stood in front of her and gave her the good news, as he stood there so freely as the only one who could help her now and to whom she was forced to turn – right then his own much deeper dependency became helplessly visible as well as a despondency of such mute heaviness that he was scarcely able to speak. His eyes turned to hers, unfree.

He tried to reassure her and actually succeeded. Not himself, however. Waking up, so to speak, after the violent rush of all that happened that afternoon, a pressure remained within him and an aftertaste of some threatening meaning in this turn of events. She had also spoken about the dreams she now had frequently, in which there was always some sort of antique Russian tea service, vivid crimson, with a sugar bowl of wild, you might say, barbaric form. Katia had come back again and again to this dream with a certain obstinacy; had she perhaps suffered some sort of mental disturbance in the midst of all this terror? He suddenly turned around in the street, walked back to the Tjurma, went to Katia again, even if this was not particularly smart, since it could draw attention. She was astonished, Jan completely confused by now. They stayed sitting close together in Katia's room for a while, in front of a small candle. When Alwersik got back, he found Stangeler waiting for him – no fewer than 38 witnesses had come forth who were prepared to give favorable testimony on Poccal's behalf.

He had to promise her repeatedly not to reveal anything, especially now, since things seemed so favorable that the captain was close to being able to come and go as he wished. Ten Austrian soldiers had gone to Blau as a delegation. The latter promised the men to see the affair through justly and benevolently, but basically conducted himself with reserve and presented a stern figure behind the thick beard which he now wore à la Trotsky. On the fifteenth of March, at noon, Stangeler visited Alwersik who was lying on the cot in his room. The slant-eyed one was clearly having trouble keeping quiet and so Alwersik pre-empted his unspoken words. He knew, he said, that the offer to be discharged expired at 6 PM that day but that was no longer relevant for him, but he, Stangeler, should take the necessary steps to get away from there, take off. Stangeler shook his head and left. On March 17 the trial against Poccal and his wife began. Blau was in charge and opened the proceedings with a short speech – not without unctuousness – to the effect that a revolutionary tribunal was not simply a hanging court and if the accused had such a preconceived idea they were in error and thought too little of the revolution. Katharina and her husband, who had obviously regained his strength, sat on chairs beside a table. Among the witnesses were Alwersik and Stangeler.

Very early in the course of the trial, mention was made of the shots that had been fired from Katia's window on the night of the fifth of January – at armed workers running by, according to the indictment. This also raised, with reference to Katia, the suspicion that there was communication between herself and her husband, who was still with the White Army marching on the city, so that the enemy commanders were being informed about activities within the city. It was also claimed that for two days after the coup Katia had provided a hiding place in her dwelling for a "White" spy and scout, at a time when the workers' council had already assumed power. The entire indictment was somewhat vague, obviously thrown together from some sort of anonymous testimony.

She rejected the entire indictment as having been dreamed up, but stated at the end, to everyone's surprise, "That I did the shooting is correct, however."

"At whom were you shooting?" asked Blau.

Katia stared straight ahead. In the bare, gray barracks-room it was now, despite the presence of more than thirty people, totally silent. Light reflected in from dirty snow on a roof across the way. The bulldog-like expression on Alwersik's face sharpened a little, his jaw muscles stood out.

"I can clarify that immediately," said Katharina Poccal with complete calm. "I fired several successive shots that night, neither at members of the Red nor of the White parties to be sure, but totally blindly, out of fear, without realizing what a critical and significant moment I had chosen for my misguided shooting. Those shots had no political significance whatever. For weeks, I had been living completely alone . . ."

"You gave up your service at the hospital at the beginning of the winter. Why did you do that?"

"Out of fear of typhus and because my nerves were giving out."

"On what did you live then?"

"I received all that was owed to my husband, who was listed as missing, provisions as well as money. I thus lived completely alone and because of the prevailing uncertain circumstances, was more and more plagued by the fear of being waylaid or robbed at night. That night I was in an extremely fearful and anxious state and suddenly thought I heard a loud noise in the back, where the door opens from the garden, as well as at the shutters in front. Whereupon, in my agitation, I began to shoot, at first into the garden, then out front. Only afterward did I realize that the whole city was in turmoil."

Her manner of speaking was rather convincing. Alwersik's eyes brightened with admiration, then he lowered his lids. Katia and he did not so much as glance at one another. His astonishment at her sudden ability to portray everything clearly and logically was boundless. It was obvious that her testimony was making a favorable impression, at least among the spectators.

Blau himself remained inscrutable as usual, but now turned to the captain with a pronouncedly friendly tone.

Koloman Poccal, who had been staring at the surface of the table up until then, now looked up and directly at the face of Hugo Blau.

"The allegation that during the sixth and seventh of January I was in communication with my wife here in the city in order to obtain military intelligence for my command is nullified by the fact that by then I had long since ceased to be a member of an army unit and was, in fact, a prisoner. You seem not to be aware of the fact that I had already been taken prisoner by the Reds in November, in the vicinity of the Taiga station, along with the first Polish convoys that were disarmed; our trains were surrounded and we were pulled out of the cars. You will be able to find a large number of witnesses among the soldiers taken prisoner at the same time I was. During the Civil War I always served with the Polish Legion and was never attached to a solely Russian unit. On the other hand, you do know that the remnant of the army that attempted to take over this city on the seventh of January consisted entirely of Russian troops. For months, my wife had not been able to obtain any information to indicate that I was alive."

His brief and precise testimony seemed to render that part of the indictment groundless. Nevertheless, it was decided to hear the testimony of the relevant witnesses at the next sitting.

The matter of mistreatment of soldiers was brought up. "Accusations of this sort are generally made against all former officers of the Kolchak army," said Blau, "and hence against you as well, Captain Poccal. But it appears to me that in this case it should be easy for you to rid yourself of the suspicion."

First it was decided to hear testimony from several of the Polish legionnaires formerly under Poccal's command at the next session. But soon afterward the Captain's past activities were brought up and his effectiveness at Novo-Nikolaevsk during the summer months of 1918. Blau looked at the clock.

"The captured Red Guards," said the captain, "were being abused in the most horrible way. The nature of their treatment was such that many died. The wounded were not cared for, the sick were beaten. At the time, I had just taken over command of the camp for Austro-Hungarian and Imperial German prisoners . . ." At this point, several of the Austrian soldiers called as witnesses yelled "bravo!" and came out with a variety of cheers in Hernals and Ottakring dialects. Blau admonished them for the disturbance. "I unfortunately had," continued the captain, "no direct influence over the affair, since the captured members of the Red Guard – Russians and foreigners – were housed in the municipal jail. There was a room there into which they put almost 250 prisoners, which amounted to barely two square meters of space apiece. The entire room was divided into small rectangles by barbed wire, so that each man literally sat in a kind of cage . . . and that considerable trouble had been taken simply to torment them. If anyone made a sudden or violent movement, he was simply shot at – every day there were several dead. Finally I succeeded in putting an end to the lunacy, after trying for a long time. The accommodations were changed and the 250 men, who literally had been squatting in their own excrement, could at least stretch out on a cot. Not much was accomplished since the constant executions went right on."

"Actually, Captain, you did far more than duty required. After all, you were really only responsible for the Austrians and Germans up in the camp," commented Blau.

Poccal kept his gaze focused on Blau's face. "That may be," he said. "but first of all, the men actually entrusted to my care had things far better, even if only in a relative sense, and secondly, it would be more or less incomprehensible to think that a free man could know about such an abomination in close proximity and not lift a hand against it. In the course of all that I had some very sad experiences. Among the captured Internationals there were several who hoped to better their situations by means of vile denunciations of their comrades. One of them even succeeded and thereafter became almost a confidante of the investigating committee in Novo-Nikolaevsk that had the task of finding out who had any sort of connection with the Reds or sympathized with them – at one point I actually crossed swords with this person. Afterwards he even found a way to slander me in my own headquarters so that they questioned my reliability and opposed my attempts to better the prisoners' lot."

"What was the name of this traitor?" asked Blau.

"He had a Czech name – Nadvoniek or something like that – but was most certainly not a Czech. Whether that was his real name I have no idea."

"Does any of you know the man?" Blau asked the Austrians.

"Ba name, sho," said one of them, "back 'en we 'eard wha' da Herr Cap'n jus said. Dat Nadvoniek din't have nawthin' to do wit' da camp up 'er, on'y daoun in taoun."

"Wasn't this Nadvoniek previously an inmate of the prison camp at Novo-Nikolaievsk?"

"Naw. S'posed tu'v come from Barna-Ul, 's whar he join'd da army, 's wha' dey sed, an'way."

"Do you know, Captain, what happened to this man afterward?"

"No. One day he just disappeared forever."

"And you have no idea?"

Poccal shrugged his shoulders and fell silent. Thereafter, no one spoke for several moments. The captain's story seemed to have made an impression, a rather oppressive one, in fact – the effect was paralyzing and hopeless to a certain extent. And thus the proceedings ended in deep silence. Blau closed by saying to the defendents,

"Patience please. You can understand that in most of the proceedings here there is more involved than in your case. I will try to reach a formal conclusion to the affair as soon as possible. Further investigations will be carried out in the interim. Assuming that these further investigations do not bring previously unknown incriminatory evidence to light, there is, in your case, Captain, the matter of whether or not enlistment in the Red Army may be offered to you at the conclusion of the proceedings." With that, there was a general pushing back of chairs. Katharina and Poccal were returned to their places of custody.

In the midst of all that, the countryside round about was now beginning to arise from the oppressiveness and storms of the winter. Just as, in the light of the rising moon, hills and forests open their eyes and gaze directly at man, so now, on milder days, steppe, river, and the sky that arches over to the forested mountains lay placidly stretched out before the beholder. Often and fleetingly, the light alternated in front of Alwersik's window; the sunshine and shadows and those sunbeams falling on the sparkling snow on far-off hilltops, and even the momentary darkness from clouds passing over the houses across the alley, all washed silently up and down the walls of that room, streaking the surfaces as the shadows rose and fell, reached the bedstead on which he lay, and then moved on. Alwersik lay there, and those days his body amounted to almost nothing but just lying there. When pressed, check on the sentries, give an order – alien words, indeed, as if he had suddenly pulled some strange object or other from his own pants pockets, held it in his hand mystified – well, who stuck that in there? Just go on dreaming – her left breast filled his hand, the woman lay against him like a soft cloud merging dimly with the border where the purple solitude indistinctly began – he could not tell clearly where that was, but from there it went inward, deeper within himself. And now she had cut herself away from him, stood on her own, spoke completely logically, and fought clearly and deliberately for her happiness – however, despite all, there remained that blurred connection somewhere, and actually everything came from that dark valley between him and Katia, every bit of guilt, but above all, this condition, in which he almost physically extended out toward her, into the office of the Tjurma.

Why read the newspapers? He scarcely read an order to the end, heaps of paper grew slowly beside the bed, untouched; now and again they had to be pushed back a little to make a place for the rapidly emptying cigarette boxes. Alwersik even took his meals that way and the orderly assigned to him, a foxy Viennese, did what he was ordered and fended off any and all annoyances, as far as he could.

Everything was already thoroughly mixed together. Katia's eternal tea service amounted, for him, to the same thing as all those rumors that referred to certain of the harsher orders from Moscow or to the concealed hand – that's about how the phrase put it – that brought about change with the flourish of a pen . . .

No, no, it would be entirely wrong and possibly harmful to visit Katia now.

Behind this whole revolution stood, as well, some face or other, which had not yet unveiled itself to him – to hell with the tea-service!! Have I gone crazy?! – he suddenly thought of eyes that gaze out beyond everything, unearthly, as it were . . .

One night, however, he sat up again and decided to tear himself loose from all this entanglement, from this net into which he'd been spun. "Yeh, tear myself loose..," he thought once again, but the words hung like an empty sack. It seemed as if there were cords wound around his head or that he was wandering in corridors – "but there must still be some possibility of seeing through some of the cracks that keep getting narrower, right?"

On the following day he went to see Katia. Spring was in the streets. Piles of snow, still lying around here and there, sparkled in the sunlight, forcing one's gaze downward, in front of the feet. – Didn't anyone understand him? He wanted to see Katia, right, Katia Poccal, in the room next to the office, morons, don't you understand Russian? The clerks all looked rather disconcerted; it was completely quiet in the extremely overheated office room. "Blau . . . ," said someone and shrugged his shoulders. Alwersik tore open the door to Katia's room. "So where is she?" he screamed and lost control of himself. One of the secretaries pulled himself together, swallowed a little, stepped forward, and informed Comrade Alwersik that Blau had turned up at midnight four days ago and ordered Katia to be taken away . . .

"Where?" screamed Alwersik hoarsely.

"To the place where many were taken at night, Comrade, probably down to the river, that's probably it."

Several men now slowly crossed themselves, their heads hanging down. "A Polish captain was also taken away, on the same night, I heard it from one of the guards," said another.

"Did Blau take any of the sentries from here with him when he had the woman taken away?"

"Yes. Blau had his own men with him, but still took several along from here."

"One of the men who went along when Katharina Poccal was taken away is to report to me, in that room, immediately," said Alwersik, now calmly and concisely. That sentence cost him so much energy that he could barely summon up the strength to walk into Katia's room and slam the door behind him. He sank down on the bed with an attack of faintness. While he was still lying there, face down, there was a thumping on the door, a soldier walked in, slammed his rifle-butt against the floor, and stood at attention."

"What's your name?" asked Jan in his confusion, for no very good reason.

"Grigor Petrovitch . . ."

" Ah, never mind – you were there?"

"Yes, Comrade, I was there again."

"Tell me, talk dammit!"

"Why, Your Excellency?" said this Grigor Petrovitch, dropping his role as a Red Army man by using such an antiquated form of address. "Would your excellency find enjoyment in something so horrible? Am I perhaps to give you pleasure by telling about it? The way people were pushed under the ice, into one of those hellish black holes near the fourth island below the railroad bridge, perhaps? I will tell you nothing, damn you – nothing at all!"

"You will!" bellowed Alwersik.

"Yes indeed, one thing, one thing I will tell you," replied this no one of a Grigor Petrovitch and riveted his blue eyes on Alwersik, "there is one thing I will say to you, you devil, so that you will be a little less happy about it, you dog that God will punish, as He will all of you , you evil enemies . . ." now he too was yelling – " that I shot, that I will tell you, even though our orders were 'Do not shoot, they must go under alive,' but I shot anyway, because I would have it so, you son of hell . . ."

"At whom? Shot at whom?" screamed Alwersik.

"At the woman of course," bellowed Grigor, " at that wretched thing of a woman you had ordered to be pushed under the ice, you blasphemer! Because that Polish captain, a few hundred paces ahead, they made him swim off into eternal bliss. Yes, yes I shot, do what you will, my ears were, despite all, still too fine for such awful screams when she saw what was going to happen to her . . . !"

"You shot her?" croaked Alwersik.

"Yes and hit what I aimed at, you accursed Red dog!" Grigor Petrovitch bellowed like a steer and now was completely beside himself. He lifted up his rifle, then slammed it down in front of Alwersik's feet with a thunderous crash. "And hit what I aimed at, what I aimed at, she was dead on the spot, absolutely dead, am I not a soldier . . . do I not know how to shoot? And now I've learned all I'm going to from you Red monsters, yes, there you have the club that shoots, you dog, if I have to go to hell for my sins, I'll carry greetings from you and all like you, so they can make a nice little fire for you, a nice little fire, but there'll be no more shooting by Grigor Petrovitch . . ." His words became incomprehensible, blended into an animal cry of pain and rage, and suddenly he went at Alwersik with his fists. At the same moment, the door sprang open and banged against the wall. In the opening stood a beardless man of about forty years of age – uniform and insignia those of a military commissar. His glance passed briefly over what was taking place, the raving soldier, the rifle that lay on the floor.

"Comrade Alwersik . . ." Alwersik stared wordlessly at the unfamiliar man.

"Comrade Alwersik, don't you know what you have to do in such a case? No? Then watch – this is indeed open mutiny, watch, this is the way!" Quick as lightning he drew his pistol and shot Grigor Petrovitch in the middle of the forehead. The soldier fell clumsily and did not move again.

"I was listening from outside – they told me that you were here in order to interrogate one of the sentries. Your name is already know to me as that of a very capable commander. Sukhovlin is mine, from Moscow. Allow me to criticize your behavior, Comrade. In the current circumstances it is quite impossible to tolerate even the slightest offense against revolutionary discipline. You not only permit a soldier of the Red Army to repudiate you, a leader, and insult the revolution, you tolerate open mutiny here as well – the man throws his weapon at your feet. You should have long since done what I just did. Be aware of that, please, and in each individual situation please keep before your eyes our overall goal, for which any sacrifice can be made without further thought."

Sukhovlin spoke easily, his gaze went beyond the room, hardly touched the dead man lying on the floor, seemed not at all to be fixed on anything close by. He saluted briefly and disappeared.

Alwersik squatted down beside Grigor. He absent-mindedly fingered the blond head, from which the cap had fallen. He finally crept to his feet again, holding onto the bed, then sat there an hour or two. Some of the men came in, took the corpse away. Alwersik was not sleeping, but it was dark in front of his open eyes, as if he had closed his lids. In this darkness a name suddenly appeared, like a dancing flame: Blau .

The lighted fuse was immediately followed by the explosion, by a sea of flames which leaped from the purple darkness, in which, up until now, there had been only the wavering outline of his torment. Now, however, the force almost blew the veins on his neck apart, now his rush from the room, out onto the street, into the sled almost resembled the haste of someone overjoyed. The coachman whipped his horse, the iron of the galloping shoe splintered the ice, Alwersik tore the weapon from the leather holster on his belt, made sure it was loaded, then shoved it into his trouser pocket, safety off. His gaze, leaping ahead, dissected streets, houses, dark figures, slanting surfaces of snow on the roofs; in the gateway of the municipal command post he almost ran down Stangeler, who was standing around there for some reason or other - and now the wet stairs, and now the offices on the second floor.

"City Commander Blau - announce me immediately,

urgent, official, do you hear?"

The sentry stared at him.

"Forward!" bellowed Jan. The guard moved out of his way and crossed himself. Jan stormed on, through the anteroom and into the waiting room. Revenge. Revenge. Tear out his guts, I'll squeeze out the shit and smear your eyesockets with it. Revenge. Revenge.

From a doorway stepped Sukhovlin.

"For whom are you looking, Comrade?"

"The City Commander."

"I am he, at present and for the forseeable future."

"Where is Comrade Blau?"

"Shot at nine this morning, by my order, out on the steppe behind the Voienni Gorodok. I came from Moscow with full powers to carry out courtmartial proceedings against Nadvoniek, alias Blau."

And now, after ease had unwillingly, but nonetheless finally, come to the body tensed for the tiger's spring and the soul bared for an orgy of revenge, the outlines of that torment fluttered feebly in the purple and the solitude within him. Alwersik had turned off the electric light. One candle after another burned down on the low table. He sat there, with the slant-eyed one opposite him. Often and fleetingly the light changed, wavered in some bit of air movement not otherwise perceptible, caused tongues of shadow to reach forward to the bed, flitted soundlessly up and down the walls of the cubicle.

Yes, there they sat, as if arrived at the very bottom of life, as if in a deep shell hole, sitting on granite, as if made of stone themselves. And they could feel neither contracted nor expanded by the multiplication sign which events had dropped in front of them; rather, they were completely limited to simply looking on. From time to time one could hear the wind as if pushed at the windows, then released them again. Then the candle flame would twitch, as if breathed on, and the wall would take on shadows.

Alwersik got up slowly, skirted the table and moved to a corner of the room. Stangeler's eyes followed him and, at the same time, the look on the slant-eyed one's face resembled that of a bolting horse.

"What's your name . . .?"croaked Jan in a quiet voice.

Then he screamed, "You!"

Stangeler jumped up, took his comrade by the shoulders. "Jan, get hold of yourself! Who're you calling. . .?"

But then he lost control himself. There was something that could be sensed now, with overwhelming and astonishing power; it was the sensation that something was puffing up suddenly, like a gigantic, black bubble, distended, ready to burst and let the abundance of the dead pour into the room from out there in the night and crush everything living. The window was dark black, as if coated with India ink on the outside. Jan and Stangeler held each other by the shoulders. Then Alwersik gradually calmed down. "Who were you calling?" whispered the student.

"Ach, no one, no one . . . Grigor, I think his name was Grigor . . ."

"Who? Who's that?"

"Ach, I don't know. An unknown soldier."

Here, however, the weight-bearing wall of time collapses in upon itself and one tall arch, stressed to the point of shattering, spans from that spring night over to this present one, as I sit here and write this. Because time is nothing and I walk out of this room – into which, like a cloud filled to bursting, the nocturnal fragrance of the gardens penetrates – into the next one and from there back into this one. There the crown of a tree reaches into the night. There the silhouette of the cathedral with its onion domes rears up against the sky like a sea-shell; so presumably that is Krasnoyarsk again. There a bat flutters by. There the slope of the park I've walked through, whose perfect, robust-soft carpet of lawn still reaches into my imagination from back then, still floods into the back of my brain, or ebbs away and flows back, as if I were pulling a long cloak behind me . . .

You look – what does all that mean? I have been physically alive for thirty-two years. Everything within me is a single torment and was never anything else. They live. He looks. You are tired. Contemplated calmly, it is – nothing.

A very few hours later, the morning was already approaching the sky's edge, strips of the horizon were burning to the east. Stangeler was awakening from a deep sleep, but still held fast, as if poured under a glass surface. Every edge of the chair was pressed deeply into his body. He saw that Alwersik was awake, standing up. The room was still almost dark. A pale, gray sheen lay in the rectangle of the window.

Stangeler recognized the significance of Alwersik's movements. The latter checked the clip in his pistol, then buckled on his belt with the weapon. When the door had shut behind Jan, the slant-eyed one tore himself out of the drunkenness of sleep: after him, but don't let him see you! The fresh air awakened him finally, after the torpor of the overheated room. Alwersik was up ahead, Stangeler following him from corner to corner. They proceed in that way in the direction of the railroad workshops, then around them to the left and up the slope toward the mountain. Here it was much harder for Stangeler to remain unnoticed. He hid in gullies, waited behind bushes. The day was coming on.

Here the countryside became flatter as it receded toward the forests, the early spring grayness of the ground still streaked and flecked by left-over snow. Alwersik made directly for the woods. Stangeler followed a curving path, and when Jan walked between the first straggling trees and underbrush, the slant-eyed one was concealed scarcely ten paces from him. Three minutes passed in complete silence. During that time, Jan stood bent over somewhat; then he reached toward his belt. But before he even had the gun entirely out of the holster, Stangeler had covered the distance in three bounds and grabbed him by the wrist. They began to wrestle immediately. Stangeler hadn't really expected anything else – he knew this Alwersik. They both put their entire strength into it and Jan, with a desperate look in his eyes, threatened to shoot and at the same time tried to point the barrel at Stangeler. Jan had the advantage, was more agile; his opponent was somewhat clumsy, but heavier. They fought there for nearly an entire minute in the dull, gray dawn of a gloomy day. Then Alwersik's left knee suddenly gave way – a reminder of a Russian bullet – he lurched forward, Stangeler tried to get the gun away from him. When that didn't work, he lashed out again and Jan sank into one of those brief periods of unconsciousness that can result from the blow of a fist to the jaw.

Stangeler squatted down beside him. In fearful haste he tore the clip from the pistol, tossed the bullets in different directions, then threw the gun far into the underbrush. Jan was already awakening.

He stood up, looked at Stangeler with eyes that were still bloodshot, but whose expression no longer fit with that fact, turned around, and walked off with a sort of jerky shuffle, across the flat meadows and toward the road, then down toward the town. Stangeler followed him to the beginning of the slope and watched him go. He saw and felt clearly from the way Alwersik was walking that he would go on living. A pernicious exhaustion came over him. He collapsed on the edge of the incline and slept.

Summer had come. Alwersik and Stangeler were relaxing on a bench on the quay, the former still in the uniform of the Red Army, with the insignia of a commander. The water lapped against the shore, the current swirled by in the evening, the islands seemed to be swimming. It was a mild summer evening. The entire quay was swarming with couples.

"Tell me, Stangeler, why you're really still here."

"You know," said the slant-eyed one.

"I've got to get out of here," said Jan dryly. He had never brought up the subject previously. "I know it could cost me my life. But regardless, I've got to. I can't live in Russia any longer."

"I'll go with you."

"Do you know what it would mean to be caught with me?"

"Yes, I know very well."

"So, shall we take off together?"

"Yes."

They started their preparations that very same evening. Standing at the station was a freight train with damaged vehicles, airplanes, and other war materials waiting to be taken back to Moscow for repair. After several days, they burrowed into the fuselage of an airplane with ample water and provisions. Alwersik had tried unsuccessfully to find any excuse to be transferred to the west on some mission which would make it possible to take Stangeler along. But Jan no longer wanted to wait patiently. He was in a hurry. And it may well be that he felt more secure doing it this way. They made it as far as Omsk without problems. There, however, their hiding place became risky because part of the military cargo was being unloaded and transferred to the local repair shops. They faked their way without tickets – they were issued only to holders of travel permits – along a further stretch of the railroad line to the west, but this turned out to be difficult, since surveillance by the authorities in that sector was unpleasantly sharp. Jan lost his patience again, pushed on, completely away from the railroad and the cities – which was understandable in his situation – and so they marched southward into the steppes and then westward, in order to get to European Russia on foot.

In those days many departed in similar ways, even before the first train convoys – which were merely talked about for the moment – really began to roll. For many of them, during the weeks and months of their wanderings, the landscape opened up once again like a massive folio volume, and many crept over its broad arched surface and finally left it – most of them, to be sure, like bookworms who had merely eaten, not read. And thus, over time, Russia released her last foreigners from the west. To those wandering homeward, the peasants along the way still offered, a thousand times over, a hospitable roof, a friendly word, and shared their bread and their milk pails with them, and asked whether their mothers were still alive back home, whether perhaps there were wives or sweethearts, or maybe even children back there in Germany who were awaiting their return. And when did they have their last letter from them? And then there were those last, memorable conversations about the sin of taking part in wars and the salvation from it through our Lord, Jesus Christ. In that way the peasants imparted to those wanderers – quickly, at the last instant, so to speak – that most necessary advice, offered in such a touching way even to many a godless one.

Stangeler and Alwersik, too, were touched by the gentle hand of the peasant and received its blessings along a large part of their way. Only in the Khirghiz regions did they lack these protectors and hosts and chose a night in a foul-smelling yurt over sleeping around a campfire far out on the steppe. And (melancholy – exhilirating!)

the soldier in both of them came to the fore, be it in the quick, purposeful, and correct movements with which they packed up their rucksacks in the mornings, or the way they toted them along, marching silently for hours, side by side. At night they drew straws to divide up the watch – before midnight, after midnight.

There they sat beside the flickering, glowing mound of dried horse or camel dung, the only means of cooking in that treeless region, and looked out into the empty distance, which, on overcast days, seemed to be cut off by a gray, iron curtain; and each one probably even studied the features of his sleeping comrade, illuminated by the flames.

Your face, approaching me, close and free . . . you, solitary in the landscape, as free as I am or a rock or tree; the handshake that has no wish to bind and yet binds and creates a bond, so independent of all those buffeting forces to which we slaves owe allegiance. Only such hands, stretched toward each other from the cages in which we beasts sit, only such hands are free, and we, the hunted, catch sight of the exalted empire of which we are an indivisible part. Should that gate open, however, then even the eastern plowman with his implement from far away can walk right beside the sad, little boy, the German farmer beside the white picket fence, the temple servant beside the one who has been waiting, and all that fuzz, that whole ball that we have spit out there, that whole sphere whirls together and becomes one and is huge – though able to be visualized, so that we can clearly see something that is wandering darkly from west to east out of that mountain of war thrown up from rubble and human bodies, making the entire horizon flare up, dark red. Yes, even that is part of it, even if we still can only see it through spaces that are narrowing again, but still persist between the individual lovers, the individual village plowmen, the individual shafts of whips, and the door to the adjoining room, now closing once again. Because that subtle longing, distributed everywhere on the opposite edge of the city, really does want more, has pushed forward and is really standing there just in front of the boundary where everything must run together to a single figure - does it not assume, here and there, for you and for me, a predestined face? Does it not flow together from its haze? How splendid it would be - and yet, at the same time, what a fall from heaven - if such a face were really to take form and spring forth once again, degenerating sidewards, so to speak, into time and flesh. But for now, its features still drift, ghostlike, along the distant horizon to the west; while here a motionless, starry sky arches over the steppe and the two men. Farewell, comrades. In you was the empire, the salvation.

Afterword

Like his fictional alter ego René Stangeler, Doderer walked out of Russia, arriving home in 1920 in a British uniform given him along the way to replace the tattered remains of what the Austro-Hungarian army had once provided. He and his fellow members of the elite 3rd Vienna Dragoons, unhorsed just before World War I by the Austrian Army's modernization program, had been captured by the Russians in 1916 while fighting as infantrymen on the Galician front and sent off to the prisoner of war camps along the Trans-Siberian Railway, where Doderer's life for the next four years was more of less simlilar to that led by his fictional characters in *The Secret of the Empire*.

The uniform was not the only break with the past. Doderer returned home firmly resolved to seek his future as a writer and with several early attempts in hand, finished while in the camps. Most of these were subsequently destroyed when their author judged them, in the light of later, less hermetic civilian existence, as "hothouse creations." In fact, even *The Secret of the Empire*, though it was published a decade later, must have fallen somewhat under this negative judgment, since its author was reluctant to have it reprinted during his lifetime. And nothing is known about the effect of those early works in convincing his parents that their son had literary talent.

What is certain, however, is that Doderer's father agreed to support him in his efforts toward a literary career, the sole condition being that the young man first attend the university and obtain his doctoral degree, which he did in the field of Viennese Renaissance history. The instinct of his canny father, a renowned and ennobled civil engineer, was correct: as "Herr Doktor," Doderer enjoyed the respect of the title-fixated Viennese far beyond what would have been justified by his early literary efforts and scanty income, receiving deferential treatment even by the tax collector. Only the "Hausverwalter," a race more closely related to the Parisian concierge than to the American building superintendent, remained immune to any implication that the Herr Doktor deserved special treatment. Doderer, in turn, reserved a particular literary venom for a group he considered snitches and enforcers of petty rules.

In fairness, however, the Hausverwalter very likely had to put up with a difficult renter. The exotic name Heimito, short for Franz Carl Heimito, Baron von Doderer, itself suggests the possibility of unusual behavior and there was sufficient of that on the way to what one critic later called "massive and occasionally eccentric independence." After his early marriage came to an end, there were occasional scurrilous goings-on in his lodgings, such as the "interviews" of a succession of obese ladies who were to serve as models for characters in one of his novels. But for the most part, his life was spartan and limited to his own neighborhood, and his eventual working habits rigorous. He began in the very early morning hours with strong coffee, powdered in a Turkish hand-grinder and cooked over a spirit lamp beside his bed – doubtless a legacy from his Turkish fellow prisoners in Siberia – then proceeded to work, sometimes in the bath tub, until at least noon. Afternoons and evenings were spent in his favorite coffee houses or restaurants, indulging in prolonged discussions or readings from his work. Photographs or recordings of the latter suggest a theatrically vigorous style and it is perhaps altogether appropriate that his favorite restaurant was "Falstaff."

His early support came from newspaper articles and stories for various magazines. An early volume of poetry was published by Erwin Haybach, an "Old Sibiriake" – a comrade from the prison camps – and the earliest novels, such as the current volume, reflected either the influence of Doderer's war experiences or that of his renaissance studies. The publication of *Every Man a Murderer* in 1938 marked his eventual arrival at a stage where recognition and material success would finally be sufficient to insure his future. At that point the Second World War intervened, Doderer was called back to the military, and served, perhaps benefiting from being older and Austrian, mostly in rear echelon areas in France and Russia. He was in Norway when the war ended, became a prisoner of war once again – this time of the British – and returned home the following year.

He kept detailed diaries all the while. They are remarkable for their near total lack of mention of the war and the circumstances in which their author found himself, containing instead philsophical musings, thoughts about the writer's craft, and long preliminary studies for what would become his future novels. Doderer described himself as "skating on the surface like a water insect," never sinking into that second reality which would eventually be gone, if one could manage to survive. His emotional reaction to the new war, however, can be implied from the vast difference in atmosphere which surrounds his short stories dealing with the two wars: the elegiac farewell to a small chateau in "Battlefield Burial" as well as the sense of relief when a court executioner exits the train in which a soldier is returning to battle in "An Encounter at Dawn." Both reveal a First World War portrayed in terms of external forces of destruction and death that might takes one's life without having eaten into the soul or having diminished self-esteem; the vision of the Second World War conveyed in "Beneath Black Stars" is one of darkness, sightless windows, twisted lives and personalities – a pervasive, distorting, evil madness that darkened and ossified even those aspects of life not directly related to the actual, armed conflict.

The war years also marked a change in the author's technique, and it is worth mentioning that two of the novels available to the American reader, *Every Man a Murderer* and *The Demons* (the former published before and the latter after the Second World War) exemplify that change. As the author noted in his diary: "'*Every Man a Murderer*' is . . . really almost more a biography than a novel. Because here there is a protagonist, from whom everything develops and the environment is construed . . . a defined world-cave appears. Lead voice and accompanying voices. Here lies the distinguishing characteristic of the biographical technique. Only with the crucial step towards counterpoint does it expand to that of the novel;

that counterpoint, namely, which immediately occurs when several different world-caves, which are, of course, arranged very differently by their inhabitants, come into relationship with one another."

The latter is what Doderer termed the novelistic technique; others have called such a work a "total novel." The dense weave of characters, events, and motives in this style – not by any means obviously related to one another – is clearly seen in *The Demons*. Here, in order to provide insight into Austria's slide towards totalitarianism that the author thought began with mob's burning of the Palace of Justice in 1927, Doderer requires the reader to live, as it were, among the various layers of Viennese society for a prolonged period before the event occurs. There is simply no helpful shortcut to understanding such things. Nor is there any guarantee that they will be understood; it is equally likely that the reader, having "been there," will conclude that it is impossible to anticipate or understand such events when one is buried in the details of one's own life.

But if there were nothing more to it than that, one would have to chew a great quantity of verbal fodder for relatively little nourishment. However, early in *The Demons*, a clue to the deeper nature of Doderer's technique is offered by one of the characters who says, "And yet, in fact you need only draw a single thread out of the fabric of life at any point you choose and the run will make a pathway across the whole, and down that wider pathway each of the other threads will become successively visible, one by one. For the whole is contained in the smallest segment of anyone's life-story. . . ." Doderer, in other words, espouses a way of comprehending life that is slow, indirect, and retrospective, rather than rapid and always forward-striving. He makes the reader stop and re-examine things normally passed by, the things of seemingly little consequence that fill most lives; but he will re-examine them, thanks to the author, through eyes that really see and comprehend and with an intellect that senses the significance of a situation and hints at motivation that the characters themselves may miss. It amounts to an almost religious reverence for the small, ordinary details of life and, indeed, for the ordinary people of life, as the author as much as tells us when he says of his comrades at the end of the current volume, "In you was the secret." And in *The Strudelhof Stairway*, which deals with the last few years before the Great War, Doderer's method culminates in an extraordinarily moving requiem for the Hapsburg Empire, an empire whose greatness depended as much on marriage as on force of arms.

For some, it can also be a troubling technique, since one may come away from the reading of one of Doderer's later novels feeling somehow enriched without being able to say quickly and succinctly how or why this has happened, a situation which nowadays may lead to a slight feeling of guilt or upset on the reader's part. Be that as it may, it is interesting that *The Secret of the Empire*, with its multiple parallel subplots that do not quite intersect, reveals Doderer experimenting quite early on with what came to be his mature technique.

Evident also in *The Secret of the Empire* is Doderer's frequent use of verbal leitmotifs, likely an early manifestation of his feeling, clearly enunciated later, that writing and composing music were very closely related activities. Indeed, the former Siberian prison camp cello player eventually even tried his hand at composing. Later, as a writer striving to manage and properly time and integrate the various subplots involving the numerous characters – a repertory troupe, actually – that people his mature novels, Doderer "composed" on large sheets of drafting paper, covering them with notes and symbols connected by arrows, all squiggling and revolving around each other like mad mandalas or Saul Steinberg drawings. Some of the later stories were termed "divertimentos" and divided up in ways reminiscent of the movements of a string quartet. And his sentences, as well, came to show strong kinship to music, becoming increasingly long, rhythmic, and complex; but, as well, they are full of alliteration, puns, and other evidences of an active sense of humor.

Regardless of what the author may have thought about the close relationship of his works to music, the richness of his visual imagery, even in the earliest works, is likely to lead the reader to conclude that Doderer was more painter than musician. Symbols leap out at every turn of the page: splintered plaster cherubs convey the destruction of an era, locomotives are the stamping, snorting bulls of fate, blackened windows the closed gates of purgatory; the open spaces, the "rooms in the forest" often referred to in the current volume, signify the empty intervals, the bare spaces in life where vision and personal revelation may occur. And during a lightning flash that illuminates one such forest space, René Stangeler is seen grinning – the very grotesque of immaturity.

In fact, Doderer was very much a word person, a thing person – a toe may turn off one of his characters, a nose may put *him* out of joint, a beard may get him into trouble, pencils accuse him of the disorder in his life, and a folded newspaper may induce a deja-vu. Small wonder then, that things, objects, are closely connected with two other aspects of his writing: his fatalism and his sense of the spirit of place, the *genius loci* , which often becomes an actor in the drama of his novels.

In *The Secret of the Empire*, the hint of something gruesome about an antique Russian tea set eventually becomes reality; and the seeming battle between intertwined railroad bridges at home in Vienna is the predictor of the civil war battles that ride the rails in Siberia. In fact, it is but a short reach to infer that the railroads themselves contributed strongly to Doderer's sense of fatalism. Some of the author's earliest memories were of the rail lines, the viaducts, and the puffing trains near the home rented by his father while he was designing and overseeing the construction of the commuter lines into Vienna. What must it have meant later, to the young Austrian soldier, to be carried off to the most memorable time and place of his life, into Siberia, by the same creatures of steel?

For the mature Doderer, the stroller who loved the every aspect of the face of Vienna, the parks, the alleys, the buildings – who even compared to a harp's note the sound generated in the overhead power wire by an approaching streetcar – places have their own invisible spirits that intervene in our lives. Sometimes they provide stage settings, coaxing forth or precipitating actions and giving them their proper significance; sometimes they are like gentle guardians who hand us on to another place or another time, or introduce us to someone who will change our lives; sometimes they are so constituted that they delay us, divert us, make us stop, contemplate what is and has been, and thus live more fully. Sometimes, like *The Strudelhof Staircase*, they do all of those things and are, as well, the mute, sad, registrants of the past.

At other times, however, Doderer seems to be saying that the stage on which our lives are eventually acted out may be less important to our development and behavior than the dim, fragmented images from the distant past we carry within us and which relate to one another in ways not easily put into words, but which emerge, like recurring melodies, to move and dominate us. And hence, sometimes, people, things, and places are able to elicit unfortunate reactions from us when they collide with those images. In his later years Doderer devoted considerable attention to pointing out the troubles caused by the inability or refusal to perceive external reality for what it is and distinguish that reality from the effect that its symbolic aspects have upon us, which in turn can lead us into a dangerous or destructive "second reality." This is clearly and humorously seen in the short story *The Trumpets of Jericho*, where the mere sight of a pensioner's nose looses a set of responses in the protagonist that leads through false accusation, blackmail, artistic stagnation, and ultimate rescue via an equal, but this time conscious, deliberate, and very literal assault on another nose.

All of these ingredients, enhanced by Doderer's extraordinary powers of memory and his extensive diaries, coalesced into a truly remarkable literary productivity beginning in the early 1950s. During the last decade of his life, his novels alone amounted to nearly 2,500 pages, quite aside from numerous short stories, "even shorter stories," and "grotesques." Despite the recognition and improved financial status that followed the novels *The Strudelhof Stairway* and *The Demons*, Doderer himself remained, as did his writings, firmly rooted in Vienna, and he continued to pursue, despite his remarriage, a relatively simple, near-bachelor's existence in the Alsergrund district, parts of which, like the stairs in the novel, had come alive, had almost become celebrities in fact, thanks to his words.

Only at the very end of his life did he stray from those precincts. Like the Englishman, Edmund Blunden, who wrote in his introduction to *Undertones of War*, "I must go over the ground again," Doderer returned – in his mind at least – to go over the ground on which he had stood some fifty years before, to Siberia. At the very end, in a losing race against death in 1966, he was reworking the themes of *The Secret of the Empire*, reshaping the events and people encountered there into a novel in his mature style, titled *der Grenzwald* ("The Border-Forest"). A comparison between these two works that mark the beginning and the end of his career provides an epigrammatic biography of Doderer's creative powers. And that last novel, fragment though it is, may well make the reader gasp – for what it is, for what it might have been.

John S. Barrett